Catherine Marsh

The Life of Arthur Vandeleur

Catherine Marsh

The Life of Arthur Vandeleur

ISBN/EAN: 9783337038922

Printed in Europe, USA, Canada, Australia, Japan

Cover: Foto ©Raphael Reischuk / pixelio.de

More available books at **www.hansebooks.com**

THE LIFE

OF

ARTHUR VANDELEUR,

Major, Royal Artillery.

BY THE AUTHOR OF

"MEMORIALS OF CAPTAIN HEDLEY VICARS," "ENGLISH HEARTS
AND ENGLISH HANDS."

NEW YORK:

ROBERT CARTER & BROTHERS,

No. 530 BROADWAY.

1862.

THESE

MEMORIALS

OF THE

HOLY LIVING AND DYING OF A SOLDIER OF THE CROSS AND OF HIS COUNTRY,

Are Dedicated,

WITH TENDER SYMPATHY

TO HER

WHO WAS THE CROWN OF HIS EARTHLY JOY,

AND WHO IS NOW LEFT TO BE HIS DEEPEST MOURNER,

AND

TO HIS ORPHANED CHILDREN;

WITH EARNEST PRAYER THAT, LIKE THEIR BELOVED FATHER, THEY MAY BE

STEADFAST IN FAITH, JOYFUL THROUGH HOPE,

AND ROOTED IN CHARITY.

" He taught the cheerfulness that still is ours,
    The sweetness that still lurks in human powers;
    If heaven be full of stars, the earth has flowers.

" His was the searching thought, the glowing mind,
    The eager will, but soon to God resign'd,—
    And, more than all, the feeling just and kind.

" His pleasures were as melodies from reeds ;
    In books, sweet music, and unselfish deeds,
    Finding immortal flowers in human weeds.

" He deem'd man's life no feverish dream of care,
    But a high pathway into freer air,
    Lit up with golden hopes and duties fair.

" He shew'd how wisdom turns its hours to years,
    Feeding the heart on joy instead of fears,
    And worships God in smiles, and not in tears.

" His thoughts were as a pyramid up-piled,
    On whose far top an angel stood and smiled ;
    Yet in is heart was he a simple child."

PREFACE.

It may be thought superfluous to add another to those records of the lives of brave and Christian soldiers which are already before the public. "Memoirs," it may be said, "like those of Sir Henry Havelock and Captain Hammond, have sufficiently answered the question, 'Can a gallant soldier be a consistent and devoted Christian?' Why, then, need another example be added to the list?"

Possibly the little book now edited may itself answer that inquiry.

It is the history of one who was a Christian, by the grace of God, from the cradle to the grave,—one whose path of shining light, trodden at the first by infant feet, although here and there indeed some shadow may have crossed it, still shone brighter and brighter unto the perfect day.

And it is the history of one who never felt that his

early consecration of himself to the service of his God, could be marred by embracing the service of his Queen and country.

That the snares of his profession were not permitted to alienate his heart from the life of faith upon the Son of God, will be proved by this brief but faithful record.

It has been compiled from the testimonies of those friends and relations who could most truly tell what Arthur Vandeleur's character was in the various stages of his life, and at the desire of her with whom alone rested the right and privilege to sacrifice the sacred privacy of her husband's thoughts and feelings and springs of action, as an offering to her God. This sacrifice has been made, in the humble hope that he, whose lips were early sealed by death, might in this manner yet speak for that Saviour whom in life he delighted to honour, "to the praise of the glory of His grace," and, through the might of the Lord and Giver of life, for the winning of many who are now dwelling in the region and shadow of death, to the kingdom of light, and life, and glory.

It is earnestly requested that each one who reads this book would pause here for a moment, to pray— GOD, OF HIS FREE MERCY, GRANT THIS, TO THE HONOUR OF HIS WELL-BELOVED SON.

The world has seen with what calm courage the Christian can meet death, amidst the fierce excitement and mortal terrors of a battle-field. But this Christian soldier met death alone, step by step steadily advancing face to face with the "last enemy," and yet "feared no evil." "There is NO DEATH," he said, "for a man who believes in the Saviour. He cannot die. He is in 'the Life,' for he is *in* JESUS; and thus he is a part of Life Eternal."

If one child should be persuaded to seek the Saviour early, by learning from this story of a Christian child, the truth of the promise, " They that seek Me early shall find Me : "—if one boy or youth should be led, in the spring-time of health and spirits, and joyful sense of life and its pleasures, to follow the example of him by whom the words were obeyed, and in whom fulfilled, " Keep innocency, and observe the thing that is just, for that shall bring a man peace at the last:"—if one young soldier or civilian, who may have more clearly recognised the duty of " believing with the heart unto righteousness " than that of " confessing with the mouth unto salvation," should be induced henceforth never more to be ashamed to confess the faith of Christ crucified, and manfully to fight under

His banner; by the narrative of this young soldier, who was "valiant for the truth upon earth," and, boldly confessing his Saviour before men, found the promise true, "Them that honour Me, I will honour:" —if one soul be brought, in humble faith and dependence upon Him "without whom nothing is strong, nothing is holy," to realise that "He that believeth on the Son of God *hath* everlasting life," and to say, "Henceforth I live! no longer a bare, self-centred existence, but, like him of whom I have read, I will live a life of faith upon the Son of God; and, redeeming the time, I will seek on every side, by my life and by my words, to persuade others to learn to know Him whom to know is life eternal, holiness eternal, happiness eternal:"—then will the writer of these memorials bless God for the call given, thus to attempt to embalm the memory of another CHRISTIAN SOLDIER.

CONTENTS.

ADDRESS BY MAJOR VANDELEUR.

CHAPTER I.

The Morning of Life.

"He walked with God in holy joy,
  Whilst yet his years were few;
The deep, glad spirit of the boy,
  To love and reverence grew."

A

ARTHUR VANDELEUR was born on the 21st of January, 1829, at Ralahine, the home of his forefathers, in the county of Clare. This place although not situated in the finest scenery of the south-west of Ireland, has still a distinct character of its own, in the beauty of the rocks amongst which it is cradled, now bold and rugged, now clothed with verdure. Ralahine possesses also the charm of historic association, in the gray ruin of an ancient castle, which still towers in melancholy pride; venerable not with age alone, but also with traditions of the gallant deeds of its hereditary possessors in the olden time.

It would be impossible to say how much the associations of his earliest years, passed in the wild scenery of Ralahine, and in playing beneath those ruins, rich with their legends of the olden time, may have aided in developing those gifts of a keen delight in the beautiful, and a romantic ideal of chivalrous courage and honour, which gave so bright a glow to the charm of Arthur Vandeleur's mind and character in after life.

He was the youngest of five children. Two of his sisters died of decline, in the first bloom of their youth; and his only brother was drowned when bathing, whilst Arthur and his surviving sister were still very young.

Little seems to have been recorded of the days of his childhood at home. But the excellence of his conduct when he was launched into school-life—his truthfulness, industry, and docility—indicate a careful and wise training of his mental and moral being in early years. That he owed this chiefly to his mother, there can be little doubt; for his father appears to have been so wholly engrossed in agricultural pursuits and speculations, that the entire charge of the family devolved upon Mrs Vandeleur.

In the year 1835, circumstances, into which it is unnecessary to enter here, induced Mrs Vandeleur to remove with her children to Limerick, where they resided during the greater part of the four succeeding years.

At that time, it was a not unfrequent custom, in Ireland, for the children of gentlemen to be sent to Sunday-schools, in order that they should share in those religious instructions which are so readily accorded to the poor, but which are, too often, out of reach of the conventional habits of the rich.

Accordingly, the little Arthur, in his sixth year, was sent every Sunday to a school in connexion with the Chapel of the Asylum for the Blind, at Limerick.

Here, by the good hand of his God upon him, he was placed under the teaching of Lieutenant Carter of the 1st Royals; a young soldier of the Cross, who, constrained by the love of Christ, consecrated some of his Sabbath hours to the task, shunned by many a professing Christian as irksome, of instilling into the minds of children the truths of the gospel of Christ.

In a letter dated May 25, 1861, Captain Carter writes: " Although twenty-six years have passed since that time, I have a very distinct recollection of the little Arthur Vandeleur of those days. There was no one in his class (which was the first) whom I can recollect so well ; indeed, I could never forget his sweet countenance, with his dark-blue, animated eyes beaming with pleasure as he took his seat amongst the little circle around me. I was deeply impressed with his evident pleasure in attending the school. He seemed much gratified when I accosted him, which I never failed to do ; and I was sure of receiving in return ' childhood's fondest look.'

"I used to attend the school in my regimental uniform, and can well believe that his very youthful mind was considerably impressed by his teacher in consequence. His lessons were always well prepared : these consisted in answering questions on a chapter, or portion of a chapter, in the New Testament, and in repeating texts of Scripture learnt by heart, proving some cardinal doctrine, such as justification by faith, the Divinity of the Saviour, &c., &c.

"After I left Limerick, my friend the Rev. Dr Carr, one of the ministers of the Blind Asylum Chapel, told me that 'little Vandeleur often used to inquire for me with earnest and grateful affection.' But since then, until this month of May 1861, I had heard nothing more of him. It would have been a great pleasure to have met him in after-life, for I am sure the endearing traits I remember must have developed into a charming character."

To the kind and earnest instructions of Captain Carter, Arthur often and thankfully referred in later years. For to those instructions he traced, under the blessing of God, the first desire of his heart, in early childhood, to give himself up to the love and service of that Saviour of whom his teacher delighted to speak to him.

> "And thankfully we praise the grace,
> Which him thus led to be
> An early seeker of that Face
> Which he should early see."

Perhaps it would be difficult to over-estimate the importance of young men of education and position coming forward to teach in Sunday schools. Their very example is a lesson which cannot be forgotten by their pupils, and the truths which they teach, with the clearness of a manly understanding, and in the warmth of a first love to their Master and only Saviour, sink down into children's hearts as good seed sown unto life eternal.

Arthur Vandeleur's first trial of school-life was made at the grammar-school at Ennis, when he was in his ninth year; but as the little boy was not happy there, his tender mother removed him at the end of three months; and in the summer of 1839, he was sent to Mr Hare's school, at Delgany, county Wicklow.

Here, the good work begun by Captain Carter was not neglected. Arthur had the privilege of being placed under the pastoral care of the late Rev. William Cleaver, Rector of Delgany, a man of God, whose name is a password to love and reverence.

"Young as we were at that time," writes one of Arthur's schoolfellows,* "we used often to speak together of the heart-searching, spiritual sermons which we heard in that church. We regularly took notes of the sermons, and were each expected to repeat a portion of the Sunday morning sermon before leaving the dinner-table.

"We boys used always to be glad when we saw Mr Cleaver, and next best to him, Mr Ormsby, one of his curates, in the preacher's seat.

"It was Mr Cleaver's custom, alternating with one of his curates, to come once a fortnight to catechise us in the Scriptures, and he had a weekly lecture to which

* Rev. E. Anderson, Hockering Rectory.

wc were frequently taken. The instructions and sermons of such good men tended, I feel sure, in no
slight degree, to produce those early impressions on
dear Arthur's mind and heart which were so lasting,
and, through God's blessing, led to such glorious results."

It was at Delgany that his military ardour was first
excited; unless, indeed, we may trace it to the impression made by the weekly sight of Captain Carter's
uniform in the Sunday-schoolroom at Limerick! A
retired captain of a Highland regiment lived in the
neighbourhood; and so great was his love of his old
military pursuits, that, for his own amusement, he
used to visit Delgany twice a-week, for the purpose of
drilling the boys, who seemed to have heartily fallen in
with his martial spirit, "so that we became," adds Mr
Anderson, "quite a disciplined corps, and attained a
very fair proficiency in company drill."

This school was broken up in the spring of 1840, in
consequence of the death of Mr Hare. In the month
of August of that year, Mrs Vandeleur placed her son
under the care of the Rev. William Spedding of Greenfield, county Cork. At this school he remained for
three years, and won golden opinions both from tutors
and companions. Here, in addition to an able school-
master, Arthur enjoyed the blessing, so rare in those
days, although, thank God, less uncommon now, of a
kind and motherly friend, not only to watch over his

physical welfare, and to sympathise with his daily little joys and sorrows, but also to foster the growth of that good seed which was springing up in his young heart.

It was Mrs Spedding's custom, at the conclusion of family worship in the evening, to allow any of the boys who chose, to remain with her, in order to repeat a few verses of some hymn which they had selected to commit to memory. Arthur always shewed peculiar pleasure in this exercise, and never failed to bring his hymn perfectly learned. To encourage the boys, Mrs Spedding gave little prizes, at the end of the half-year, to those who could best repeat the greatest number of hymns; and Arthur invariably obtained the first prize in his class. He was by this means laying up in his memory a rich store, from which, in after years, he was enabled so frequently to speak to himself, "in psalms, and hymns, and spiritual songs, singing and making melody in his heart to the Lord." And to this, indeed, much may have been owing of his eminent possession of that spiritual mind "which is life and peace," and of that overflowing gratefulness of heart which made his whole life a psalm of thanksgiving unto his God.

In alluding to his school-days at Greenfield, Mrs Spedding writes:—"During the three years Arthur Vandeleur spent with us, he was beloved by Mr Spedding and all his tutors, for his peculiarly affectionate and gentle disposition; which also made him a great favourite with his schoolfellows. He possessed both talents and industry; so that he gave little trouble to his teachers, to please whom seemed to be his constant desire. Mr Spedding says he does not remember ever having been obliged to find fault with him."

The same little light which had shone in his home, and at Delgany, burned brightly at the Greenfield school.

"When quite a little boy," writes his only surviving sister, "he was always very fond of reading the Bible. And when he went to school at Greenfield in his twelfth year, he used regularly to retire to his room for this purpose and for prayer, during the half-hour granted for recreation after breakfast. At first he was ridiculed and even persecuted on this account by some of his companions; but, by and by, his steadfastness induced two or three to follow his example, and then by degrees more joined them, until at last the numbers so increased as to cause them to be missed from the playground by Mr Spedding. After some considerable search, he found them, to his great surprise and gratification, assembled on their knees round Arthur, who was praying with them."*

An early friend,† in alluding to this circumstance, says:—" As long as Arthur remained at the school, this prayer-meeting was sustained, and continued to prosper."

* The same fact is recorded by Mrs Spedding
† The Rev. George Pakenham Despard.

Shortly after he arrived at Greenfield, he had the pleasure, keenly enjoyed by a heart so alive to friendship and affection, of being joined there by the beloved companion of his days at Delgany. Mr Anderson writes :—

"I followed him to Greenfield on the 17th of August, and can never forget the hearty welcome he gave me, as he ran to meet me. He had a wonderfully bright and cheerful countenance, which was very delightful to see, and seldom failed to shed some of its own light over the faces of those who looked upon it.

"Arthur was always very attentive to his studies; but though diligent in school-hours, there was no boy who entered with more spirit into the games than he did.

"I do not remember one instance in which he received or deserved punishment for ill conduct; and very seldom did he receive any correction on account of his lessons; although our excellent master quite carried out the directions of Solomon; and cannot be accused of having spared the rod!"

Another of his schoolfellows thus writes :* "I have a distinct recollection of Arthur Vandeleur as a play-fellow. His disposition was kindly yet sensitive; his temper was quick, but not calculated to provoke. I thought him very good-looking, and careful of his personal appearance. I never knew him connected

* The Rev. Henry O'Donnell.

with anything vicious; on the contrary, I regarded him as a boy incapable of corrupting influence. I valued his friendship because he was in every way a superior boy, and an improving companion. When we were together we did not commit ourselves to any of the besetting sins of boys, such as idleness, malicious mischief, untruthfulness, or disobedience. I was not at all surprised to find, by the Memoir of the late Captain Hedley Vicars, that Major Vandeleur had become one of those who fought under a more glorious flag than that of any temporal monarch, that he had enlisted as a soldier of the Cross of Christ. My acquaintance with him in his boyhood left this impression on my mind, that if he professed to live in Christ, that profession could not fail to be unquestionably sincere."

CHAPTER II.

The First Sorrow.

"In childhood's hour I lingered near
  The hallowed seat with listening ear;
  And gentle words that mother would give,
  To fit me to die, and to teach me to live.
  She taught me that shame would never betide
  With truth for my creed, and God for my guide
  And I almost worshipped her as she smiled,
  And turned from her Bible to bless her child."

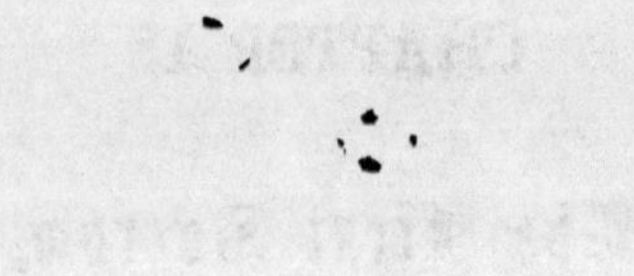

A CLOUD was now about to darken the sunny pathway of Arthur Vandeleur's young life; the shadow of which, although traced more dimly, as time brought him new hopes, new loves, new joys, had not vanished all away before he had himself entered " the valley of the shadow of death."

Grief for the loss of her elder children, and a life-sorrow which was even more deeply-seated, had preyed upon Mrs Vandeleur's delicate constitution, until at length she sank into a lingering decline, and died in the month of June, 1843.

It was in watching by his mother in many an hour of her weakness and suffering, and in seeking to soothe her sorrows, that the warm affection of Arthur's boyish heart ripened into that delicate yet intense sympathy which, in the friendships of his after years, mingled an almost womanly tenderness with the strength of a manly mind and character. One felt that, earlier or later, there had been a deep well sunk in the ground of his heart, from which such pure, fresh fountains of affection had sprung up.

Often would he sit by his mother's side, and smooth-
ing her hand in his, gaze upon her worn face, and
into her sorrowful eyes, until his own overflowed with
tears ; whilst fondly and fervently he pleaded with her
to tell him every source of her trouble. But of her
deepest grief, she could not as a wife speak to her
child, one with her though he was in every other
feeling.

But although that wound lay too deep for healing,
the hopefulness of her son's buoyant youth and happy
temperament had a sustaining and a cheering power,
as he gently strove to assure her of his belief in days
of health and happiness still in store—fond hopes of
sanguine boyhood, too soon to be destroyed by the
dread reality of death !

This love for his mother, with the memory of her
love for him, was destined to be like a guardian-angel
to Arthur, even when her earthly presence had long
been withdrawn. No lapse of time seemed to have
power to lessen its tender and holy influence.

"To the last," writes one whose heart was the
trusted depository of his thoughts and feelings, "to
the last, he cherished the little book of Prayers and
Promises, which had been one of her favourite companions, and delighted in repeating the hymns she
loved."

And well do I remember the deep emotion with
which he spoke to me of the blessing granted through

her dying words to him, when he was himself within four days of meeting her again in glory.

Notwithstanding the tender and watchful care which Mrs Vandeleur had bestowed upon the moral training of her son, she saw, when the light of eternity was streaming over her past life, that, whilst pruning the tendrils, she had missed the root of the matter. This was a subject of deep regret to her throughout her dying illness; and, redeeming the time which yet remained, she sought to lead her child to Him who is "the Way, the Truth, and the Life" of all godliness.

At their last parting (for she died whilst Arthur was at school) she laid her hand upon the head of her precious boy, and entreated him to seek with his whole heart that Saviour, whose gracious forgiving love she was then learning to realise.

She took from the young truthful lips so dear to her, a solemn promise, that as long as he lived he would never allow a day to pass without reading a chapter in his Bible, with prayer; and that, in every hour of temptation, he would pray to his Saviour for grace and strength to resist and to overcome.

With an earnestness only less intense than her own, Arthur gave the promise; and every day of his after life, save those passed in the unconsciousness of fever, witnessed its faithful fulfilment.

CHAPTER III

Clouds and Sunshine.

" Cometh sunshine after rain,
    After mourning joy again,
  After heavy, bitter grief
    Dawneth surely sweet relief ;
  And my soul, who from her height
  Sank to realms of woe and night,
  Wingeth now to heaven her flight."

WITH his mother had departed the solitary influence which might have led Arthur Vandeleur to fix upon a less wandering life than that of a soldier. His early fancies for the military profession, no longer receiving any check from the considerate tenderness of his filial affection, now resolved themselves into a decided choice.

A nomination to the Royal Artillery having been procured for him by the late Lord Fitzgerald and Vesey, he was placed by his guardian at Mr Miller's academy at Woolwich, where his studies were conducted with a view to his future profession.

He passed the examination for his cadetship, successfully; and in his sixteenth year he was admitted into the Royal Academy.

Similar trials awaited him here to those which he had encountered at school. "But he exhibited," writes his early friend, Mr Despard, "the same faithfulness; and in the end gained the same respect. In this, and in the more stirring part of his life, I need scarcely tell you, he continued faithful to the promise he had given to his dying mother. Nor need I say how eminently his stability of Christian principle, his growth in grace, and his powers of usefulness, are to be attributed to the honour he put upon the Word of God, and to his habit of daily meditating upon it.

"He triumphed, in early life, over that false shame which the young often entertain on the subject of personal religion in the presence of their companions; and the result was a strength of character, an inflexibility of purpose, and a consistency of life, which none of the trials nor temptations of his professional career, however formidable, were able to destroy."

When referring to this period of his youth, only five days before his death, Arthur Vandeleur remarked :— "The Royal Academy was a vortex of iniquity at that time.   At once, on entering it, I saw what was before me—either to go all lengths in sin, or to make a stand on the Lord's side.   But I was very young then, not sixteen; and I felt utterly unequal to standing alone. Suddenly, I remembered my mother's farewell words to me, the last time we parted, shortly before her death :— 'Put your trust in your God and Saviour,' she said; 'keep close to Him; and He will keep you and sustain you in every temptation and trial of your future life.'

"I remembered this, and the promise I had given her; and made my choice for her God and mine—her Saviour and mine.   And, oh, how faithful, how merciful, how forgiving, have I found Him to be!   How

He has borne with my shortcomings and sins; and has never, never forsaken me!"

Once, only once, in the course of his life, and that was during his residence in the Academy, did he wilfully lead another into sin and folly. To his dying day, the remembrance of this was anguish to his soul. He repeatedly alluded to it—in hours of health as well as in those of sickness—in conversation with one who was nearest and dearest to his heart, and who loved him only the more devotedly for his truthful and confiding transparency. "I led him on," he would exclaim; "and now I cannot win him back! I have not even been able to trace his course. And what, if, by encouragement to one sin, I may have given an impetus to an immortal soul, in a downward course, which may end in everlasting misery!"

It may have been owing to the enduring remembrance of this sin against a brother's soul, so deeply impressed upon the tender ground of an unseared conscience, that Arthur Vandeleur, in his years of manhood, was known to plead so frequently in prayer, these petitions of the royal Psalmist, "Remember not the sin of my youth, nor my transgressions; but according to thy mercy remember thou me for thy goodness' sake, O Lord." "Keep back thy servant from presumptuous sins: let them not have dominion over me; then shall I be upright, and I shall be innocent from the great transgression."

In allusion to the time passed at the Academy, he thus wrote in his diary some months after he had re-turned to Woolwich as a commissioned officer :—

"Oh, my God! Thou hast watched over me, and hast strengthened me to resist the varied and subtle assaults of my dreadful enemy.　Thou didst enable me to resist, in some measure, the temptations to which I was exposed at the Royal Academy.　I desire to render Thee all the glory; for what am I but a vile, miserable creature, not worthy of Thy notice, O great and good God!"

A brother officer[*] of Arthur Vandeleur's, who was a cadet at the same time that he was, and who has of late years not only been brought to the Saviour himself, but has likewise been greatly owned and honoured of God in winning others to his Redeemer, thus writes, in answer to a request that he would furnish some details of Arthur's daily life at this period :—

"Alas! I cannot help you as I would; for, when Arthur Vandeleur, at the Academy, was confessing Christ, under most trying circumstances, I was living in wilful sin; consequently, I had but few opportunities of knowing anything of his inward life.　I only saw and despised *that* in the outward life, which I afterwards learned, by the grace of God, to love and honour."

[*] Captain Orr, R.A.

CHAPTER IV.

Onward and Upward.

"Onward for the glorious prize,
Onward yet;
Straight and clear before thine eyes
In the homeward pathway lies:
Rest is not beneath the skies;
Onward yet.

"Onward till the dawn of day;
Onward yet:
Tarry not, around thy way
Danger lies: oh! fear to stay;
Rouse, then, Christian, watch and pray:
Onward yet."

His course of military education successfully completed, and his commission obtained, Arthur was now at liberty to enjoy himself amongst his friends in Ireland for a short time, previous to his joining the regiment. This "leave" was chiefly spent at the delightful home of his kind relative and guardian, James Molony, Esq. of Kiltanon, county Clare. Here he enjoyed all the pleasures of country life in a scene of singular beauty, combined with the happiness of a home, in the society of his young cousins and their honoured parents.

Such society had ever a peculiar charm for him, and few persons had a more remarkable power than he possessed, of throwing himself into the very heart of a home-circle; of becoming one with its every interest, and even reckoned among its most cherished members. But at Kiltanon, there was a centre of deeper feeling, from which a ray of distant hope diverged, pointing towards another home in years of coming manhood—a hope held indeed in a trembling heart, but with a grasp of manly vigour and unvarying constancy. Vain were the warnings that from these dreams he must one day awaken to disappointment. Arthur Vandeleur's was just the knightly character to

> " Cherish a dangerous hope,
> Dearer for danger."

And in this young heart, not only was there a strength of purpose to battle with difficulties, but also a realising faith that every event of life was in the hands of an Almighty Father; assuring him that if this bright dream were indeed the blessing he believed, no earthly obstacle should prevent its fulfilment.

About this time, or rather almost immediately upon quitting the Academy, he commenced writing a diary, which he kept with great regularity. Amidst the simple records of a young man's amusements, interests, and duties, it is remarkable to find so much unsparing self-investigation, watchful circumspection, and warm religious feeling, as may be traced in its pages :—

"*Sunday, September 26th*, 1847.—I am shortly to be commissioned, and to commence a new career. Yes; then all restrictions which have hitherto bound me will be withdrawn, and I may be said to be my own master. But no; thanks be to God, I have a Master in heaven, and a very merciful, kind, and indulgent Master He is. Shall I not, then, serve Him with reverence and godly fear? Yes; I will serve Him with all my strength, and soul, and spirit; and not

only serve, but love and honour Him. But who am
I that say, 'I will do this?' or what power have I to do
anything of myself? None! trusting in my own
strength. But my earnest prayer is, that God would
give me such a measure of His grace and Holy Spirit,
that I may glorify Him in my body and in my spirit,
which are His."

"*Tuesday, October 5th.*—The text for the day is,
'My soul doth magnify the Lord.' Truly it does. Oh,
may I be enabled to glorify Thee for Thine infinite
mercies; but especially for bringing my soul 'out of
darkness to light, from the power of Satan unto God!'

"Much has occurred since I last wrote. The public
examination at Woolwich, getting my commission, and
travelling from Woolwich here, (Kiltanon). Thou
hast watched over me, O my heavenly, holy Father—
yes, my FATHER, for such Thou hast condescended to
call Thyself in Thy holy Word. Hold me up by Thy
providence; keep me by Thy power; and, above all,
teach me to know and love Thee as much as my frail
nature is capable of; for my Redeemer's sake. Amen."

"*Friday, 8th.*—Glorious Lord God, who knowest
every thought of my heart, enable me to realise Thy
presence at all times; let me ever be fearful of offend-
ing Thee, from whom I have received so many signal
mercies, and strive to shew forth my gratitude both
with my mouth and by my daily actions. . . . . Oh,
have mercy upon this country, and I beseech Thee pre-

serve those whom I love from all evil. Keep them from the deadly shot of the cowardly assassin, and from all spiritual and bodily injury. Oh, let Thine eye be ever over us, for Jesus Christ's sake. Amen."

"*Friday, 22nd.*—I left dear Kiltanon on Monday last. Vouchsafe, O God, Lord of heaven and earth, to watch over one whom I love. Keep her as the apple of Thine eye; hide her from all that might harm or grieve her, under the shadow of Thy wing.

"*Saturday, 23rd.*—Had a long argument with one of my relations about the uselessness of my ever thinking of M—— as a wife; but although all things are now apparently against it, my trust is in the infinite mercy of my God: and if it be His will that my prayers should be answered, He can, by His almighty power, cause such to be the case; and this I most earnestly beg of Him for the sake of His dear Son. But if, on the other hand, He knows it to be *best* that the desire of my heart should not be granted, then enable me, O God, to say from the bottom of my heart, ' Thy will be done.'

> ' If Thou shouldst call me to resign
> What most I prized, it ne'er was mine;
> I only yield Thee what was Thine;
> Thy will be done.'

"*October 23rd.*—O great and glorious Jehovah, hast Thou already answered one of my prayers, and so glorified Thy servant in making me the humble instrument in Thy hands of shewing to my dear aunt the way of salvation; of pointing out to her Christ crucified as her atonement, and of leading her to Thee as her reconciled Father! Thy works are unsearchable and past finding out. Put Thy Holy Spirit into my heart in much more abundant measure, that He may shew me what I ought to speak; help me to set before my dear aunt, Jesus Christ and Him crucified, as 'the Way, the Truth, and the Life;' to shew her that, through His merits, she may approach boldly to the throne of grace, to obtain mercy, and find grace to help in every time of need; and so draw her close to Thee that she may rest her entire hopes upon Thy blessed Son.

"*Sunday,* 24*th.*—How easy is it to speak and write seriously, compared to what it is to think seriously! How difficult it is to resist the tempter, and how well Satan knows every person's weakest points! O gracious Saviour, put Thy Holy Spirit into my heart, that He may enable me to resist Satan in whatever disguise he presents himself. Grant, I beseech Thee, that I may grow in grace, and in the knowledge of my Lord and Saviour Jesus Christ. Let me learn to resist the devil more; that, gaining daily more experience under the banner of my dear Saviour, I may at last be able to interpose the 'shield of faith' before every dart which my malignant and active enemy can hurl at my soul.

"*October, Monday,* 25*th.*—This evening I have been

much delighted with some examples of Divine grace in the Army and Navy, (which I read of in a book called 'The Church in the Army,') particularly by that of a young midshipman who heard the truth one evening, and, immediately upon hearing it, God brought it home with such power to his soul that he, that very night, 're-joiced with joy unspeakable and full of glory.' Would to God that I might be like him! Oh, give me, gracious God, that 'peace which passeth understanding, and which the world can neither give nor take away.' For in Thee, O Lord, do I trust; yea, all my hope is in the all-sufficient merits of my Redeemer. I do heartily repent me of my former sins, and utterly abhor them. I believe that thou hast pardoned them, for my Saviour's sake. Then, O God, open Thou my lips, that my mouth may shew forth Thy praise. The greatest desire of my heart is, that Thou wouldst permit me to speak before men to Thy honour and glory. Yea, O Lord, let me glorify Thee, both in my body and in my spirit, which are Thine. Am I Thine? Wilt Thou have me, unworthy me, for Thy servant? Oh, what an honour dost Thou confer on me, to be a servant of that great and glorious God who dwelleth in eternity, whose name is 'Jehovah'! Oh, teach me to value this aright! Put Thy grace and strength into my heart, and grant me a most abundant measure of Thy Holy Spirit, that I may confess Thee before all men, and not be ashamed."

*　　*　　*　　*　　*　　*

"*October 27th.*—For how much have I to be thankful to my gracious God! Truly He has watched over me for good, and raised up dear kind Mr Molony to be my guardian, when I was most in need of his wise and kind care. And *has* he not been a good and kind guardian to me? Yes, truly—the best kindest, and most judicious friend. And my mouth shall praise Thee, O my God, for this gift, with joyful lips; and may I set forth Thy praise with my life also!

"*October 28th.*—Went to a quiet little party at Mrs C——'s, where we were silly enough to play small plays; but we enjoyed ourselves immensely, laughing very heartily, and returned home at about half-past eleven o'clock.

"I took a long walk to Monastereven to-day, and enjoyed some very sweet communion with my God; for which I give Him thanks and praise. Oh, what honour Thou didst confer upon me this day, good Lord, in permitting me to see so much of Thy wonderful love towards mankind, in giving up Thine only Son to die that we might live, the just for the unjust, that He might bring us to God!

*　　*　　.　　*　　*　　*　　*

"*October 29th.*—How hard it is to strive between the world and your conscience! 'Ye CANNOT serve God and mammon.' Oh, my gracious God, let me not halt between two opinions! Let me take up my cross daily to follow Thee, and joyfully fight under Christ's banner against the world, the flesh, and the devil!"

"*October 31st.*—This day I partook of that blessed sacrament of which Christ Himself hath said, 'Do this in remembrance of me.'

"Oh, let me never forget, gracious Saviour, that I have given up myself to Thee, to be Thy zealous and devoted follower here on earth; and I trust, through Thy merits, also to be a partaker of those joys which are at Thy right hand for evermore. May I never disgrace Thee or that blessed cause in which I have embarked; but be so endued with grace and power from on high, that I may stand out boldly for the cause of truth, and not be afraid of, or be put to silence by, the scorn of a frowning world!

"*November 1st, Monday.*—Went out shooting this morning, with Trevor Hamilton, on Derryleague bog. This evening we went to a quadrille party, and returned home at a reasonable hour. It will not do for me to go to all these parties. And as, if I go to one, I must go to all, I must give up going to any. O my God, why halt I between two opinions? Let me choose to follow Thee, despite all the assaults of my adversary the devil! I find, by sad experience, that he always attacks me on my weakest side; and, grieved I am to say, he too often succeeds. Oh, strengthen me by Thy might in the inner man."

* * * * * *

"*November 6th.*—Good and merciful Lord God, I bless Thy holy name for permitting me daily to have such an opportunity of intercourse with Thee as Thou didst graciously afford by making me to keep this journal. Oh, bring me close to Thee, day by day; and let me hold sweet communion with my own gracious Saviour, Redeemer, Shepherd, and Friend, daily—nay, hourly—by faith. Oh, let me rejoice in Thee. Shew me more of the vanity and folly of this perishing world, that I may gradually and effectually be weaned from placing either my hopes or my happiness upon it. No; I will have my all in Thee—all my affections, all my wishes, all my hopes, centred in Thee, and in Thee alone!"

"*November 8th.*—Began the day very badly, by getting up late. Pardon my sinful idleness, O God, for my Saviour's sake, and put away *all* my transgressions

"Went out shooting in the afternoon. In the evening wrote a letter to Carden, and read 'Church in the Army.' Oh, how wicked is my heart still! The old man still clings to me with fearful tenacity. Come, then, gracious Holy Spirit, into my heart, and enable me to give it up wholly to God, for Satan still struggles for possession. Yes, Lord, I feel him now. Oh, make him let go his grasp! Keep me close under the shadow of Thy wing, for there and there only shall I be secure from his murderous darts.

> 'O Holy Saviour, friend unseen,
> Since on Thine arm Thou bidst me lean,
> Help me, throughout life's varying scene,
> By faith to cling to Thee.
>
> 'Blest with this fellowship divine,
> Take what Thou wilt, I all resign;
> While as the branches to the vine,
> Saviour, I cling to Thee.
>
> An exile now, fatigued, opprest,
> E'en here I find a place of rest,
> A captive still, but not unblest,
> While I can cling to Thee.
>
> 'Blest be my lot, whate'er befall,
> Who can affright, or who appal?
> While as my God, my Rock, my All,
> Saviour, I cling to Thee.'"

In alluding to a painful conversation with an aged relative, who was at that time opposed to the dearest earthly wish of his heart, he writes:—

"She is nervous and easily excited. But she is a dear, and most kind creature, and I am very fond of her; I must endeavour to be more cautious how I speak on certain topics to her, as it is very easy to hurt her feelings."

"*November* 13*th.*—This evening, went to dine at Mr ——'s, and enjoyed the evening very much indeed; because they were all so kind and agreeable, and also because we spent our time in quiet, rational conversation, like creatures endowed with understanding, which certainly is much better than dancing and skipping about, as is generally the way at parties. I met a man there who *appeared* to me to be extremely conceited. How completely conceit veils all the good qualities a person may possess, and makes a man almost unbearable. Oh, may I never become conceited ! And what have I got to be conceited about ? Nothing; and less than nothing, for I am a grievous sinner, who cannot fulfil the law of God for a single day. Then away with conceit, away with pride, which is intolerable, and let me walk *humbly* with my God !"

Towards the close of November, 1847, Arthur Vandelcur joined the regiment, at the Royal Artillery Barracks, Woolwich Common. He entered upon his life as a soldier, with an earnest desire thoroughly to fulfil the duties of a profession to which he was, from first to last, ardently attached ; and with fervent prayers that he might be enabled to witness a good confession for his Divine Lord and Master ; and to glorify Him in his daily life. This is expressed in the first entry of his journal, on his return to Woolwich, as a commissioned officer :—

" *Monday, November 29th,* 1847.—So here I am, through the mercy of my good God, comfortably settled in my quarters in the Royal Artillery Barracks. O my God, open Thou my lips, that my mouth may shew forth Thy praise. Lord, I am Thy servant; let me rejoice that

Thou hast taken me into Thy service.   My humble prayer to Thee is, that Thou wouldst give me strength of mind and courage in an abundant measure; that Thy Holy Spirit may enable me to resist, without flinching, the laughing scoff of an ungodly world. Yea, Lord, why should I be ashamed to own that Thou hast chosen me; that I am an adopted son of that great and glorious God who inhabiteth eternity. Oh, teach me to rejoice, and to bless Thee for having made me 'an heir of God, and a joint-heir with Christ.' What infinite love and condescension! Oh, for ever will I praise and magnify Thy holy name, which alone is worthy to be praised and had in honour! To Thee will I give glory, both here and throughout the endless ages hereafter."

And on the first Sabbath following this new era in his life, we find him writing, "Gracious and Holy Spirit, come with power to my soul, and warm it with love to my dear, my own Saviour. Oh, shew to my heart His gracious image, that I may love Him with an intense affection!"

That these holy aspirations received an abundant answer, we are assured by the testimony of those who knew him best at that time.

Whilst taking an eager interest in acquiring the knowledge requisite for distinguishing himself in the noble branch of the service, to which he belonged; and, at the same time, entering with light-hearted gaiety into many of the amusements and interests of his brother officers, he still diligently persevered in keeping and recording, a daily watch over his thoughts, words, and conduct, "as one who must give account." This will be seen in the extracts which follow :—

"*Monday, December 6th.*—Broken off drill to-day by Colonel Cruttendon, having just been a fortnight at it. Been employed writing out the local standing orders all the evening since mess.

"For how much quietness and comfort in my new profession have I to be thankful! Yes, truly, my God has been very merciful to me. He has upheld me through all the slippery paths that I have walked in, and well may I say with David, 'When my foot slipped, Thy mercy, O Lord, held me up.'"

"*Wednesday, December 15th.*—Played seventeen games of racket to-day, and worked myself very hard. Went in the evening to De Havilland's room, and met there Bruce, who is a great friend of mine, and whom I like very much. He fears and loves Thee, O God, as far as my shortsightedness can see. I beseech Thee, gracious Lord God, to give him a much more abundant measure of Thy grace and Holy Spirit, to make him fear and love Thee much more than he now does. May he be a burning and a shining light in Thy true Church!"

At this time, Arthur had not only the privilege of hearing the gospel of Christ clearly preached in the Barrack chapel; but also he deeply enjoyed attending the ministry of the Rev. Capel Molyneux, then Incumbent of an Episcopal chapel at Woolwich. Mr Molyneux's gifts of eloquence and powerful reasoning were peculiarly calculated to fascinate a mind at once so impressionable and so logical as Arthur Vandeleur's: whilst his faith was nourished and strengthened by the grand yet simple Truth which the preacher taught, of a free pardon offered by a holy GOD to sinful man, through the atoning death of His Son; "one Sacrifice for sins for ever,"

Several extracts from Mr Molyneux's sermons appear in Arthur's journal. They are chiefly marked by a practical character, and were evidently applied by his honest heart to his daily life and conversation. The following is given as a specimen :—

"*Sunday, January 2nd*, 1848.—Heard this evening, from Mr Molyneux, a most beautiful sermon. His text was, 'Giving all diligence, add to your faith,' (2 Peter i. 5.) He shewed us the value of time; and how we ought to give all diligence to redeem even those two or three minutes which we continually waste; and how much good might thereby be effected. He also shewed us how sinful we are, (and I feel it to be most true as regards myself,) in giving our worldly concerns the preference above the time given to our God : how, in the morning, if we get up rather late, we slur over our prayers, and perhaps hurry through a chapter in the Bible, in order to get to our worldly business in good time; and in the evening, if we feel drowsy, how we again slur them over, in order that we may get to sleep. Now, O Lord God, I beseech Thee not to let this be my case any more, but enable me to redeem my spare moments to read Thy holy Word with reverence and devotion; and to meditate practically thereon, and also to pray to Thee with that earnestness and sincerity which Thou by Thy Holy Spirit canst alone enable me to do."

" *Wednesday, January 5th*, 1848.—Played a good deal at rackets to-day, and two games of chess with De Havilland. In the evening, went, very much against my inclination, to play a game of billiards with B—— and A——, and lost my temper in a great measure, which, besides making me the laughing-stock of my companions, was very wrong in the sight of that great God whose eyes are always upon me, and who sees into the most inmost recesses of my heart. B—— afterwards asked pardon of me; and when I was coming over to my room, asked me to read a little prayer on meekness of temper. O God Almighty, pardon my sin this night. Against Thee have I sinned, and done this evil in Thy sight. Oh, pardon me, I beseech Thee, for the sake of Thy dear Son. Oh, intercede for me, blessed Saviour! Thou wast tempted like as I have been, and yet Thou wast without sin. Thou knowest all my infirmities, and the ignorance of my heart; and still Thou lovest me. May I ever return Thy love. Enable me to put a guard over my temper; and to watch, and steadfastly to strive against, all occasions of evil."

"*January* 12*th.*—Went twice to the gymnasium to-day, to learn the sword-exercise and fencing, also the riding-school and battalion duty. Went round the coffees at five o'clock. Got a newspaper from Ireland, and spent the greater part of the evening in reading it; particularly interested in a letter of the Duke's on the National Defences. On guard in the arsenal with Captain G——; had severe cold and headache all day; visited the boring department in the arsenal, and inspected the enlarging of the bore of brass guns."

"*January* 18*th.*—Came up from guard at twelve o'clock. Played a game of billiards with Dickson for an hour. Afterwards went to the gymnasium, and remained practising fencing and gymnastics till time to dress for mess; after mess, very tired and sleepy, which occasioned me to lose the whole evening.

"Oh my dear Saviour, do not I owe Thee the best part of my time, and yet how little do I give Thee! Does not Thy great love towards me, which Thou dost manifest every day, shew me that I ought to live for Thy glory, and for it alone; and yet how far is this from being the case! Oh, pardon me, my beloved Saviour!

Do put into my heart a greater desire for Thy glory; and enable me to give up much more of my time to Thy service, and to studying Thy blessed Word. Oh, put into my heart a steadfast resolution so to do, and I shall sing of Thy mercies and of Thy love for ever and ever."

"*January* 21*st*.—My nineteenth birthday. . . . . Oh, my God, Thou who hast brought me to the commencement of a new year in my life; Thou who hast kept me in health and safety during that which is past; let Thy Fatherly care watch over me during the year which I am now commencing; so that if it be Thy holy will I should see the close of it, grant that it may find me far advanced on the road to heaven. Come, come, Holy Spirit, and aid me by Thy mighty power in all my efforts to lead a more holy and consistent life. How much is there to be corrected, how much to be struggled with, how much to be overcome! I need an entirely new heart; for mine is so utterly vile, so ready to do all that Satan wishes; so full of sin, of cowardice, and of foolishness, that I cannot keep it any longer. I will have a new one: give it to me at once, O God;—a heart that will love Thee supremely,

> ' A heart resign'd, submissive, meek,
> My dear Redeemer's throne,
> Where only Christ is heard to speak,
> Where Jesus reigns alone.'

Yes, that is the heart I will have ; give it to me, give it to me, O God, for the sake of Thy dear Son, Jesus Christ ; for hast Thou not said, 'A new heart will I give you,' and 'Ask, and ye shall receive.' "

"*Sunday, January 30th.*—This afternoon I finished reading 'Mason on Self-Knowledge.' I find it a very profitable book ; for it has opened to me quite a new way of examining my own heart : and may my beloved Saviour, by the Holy Spirit, grant that I may be enabled to search into my vile heart, and to root out all that wickedness which lies so strongly embedded at the bottom of it. Spent the early part of the evening very unprofitably, by sleeping when I might have been reading and meditating on Thy Holy Word. Pardon, pardon, O Almighty Father, my many sins and infirmities, and give me moral courage and determination that, when I know a thing to be right, I may accomplish it, and not allow Satan to triumph over me in any way."

"*February 1st.*—Finished reading the history of the Seven Years' War in Germany ; by which I have acquired some knowledge of the relations of the several powers of Europe to each other towards the close of the last century.

"*February 2nd.*—Before I left the arsenal to-day I visited the foundry and boring departments, and inspected the method of getting the correct curve for the swell of the muzzle of a brass gun."

In the course of this journal we find occasional allusions to the billiard-table, which Arthur was beginning to find an unprofitable amusement; but it was not until after many struggles, and much prayer for grace and strength, that he was enabled entirely to give it up.

"*February 4th.*—Went to the billiard-room, and very foolishly played a game of pool, whereby I lost a good deal of money. I have no doubt it was wisely ordered, that I might not get fond of the game. Oh, have I not had a lesson to prevent me from getting into the habit of gambling. Save me from it. Save me from it, O my God.

"*5th.*—I went to the billiard-room again, and played a game of pool with some of the best players in the garrison, and won some money. I have fully determined in my own mind I will not play any more pool, as I feel that it excites me too much, and may God, by the help of His Holy Spirit, enable me to keep this resolution sacredly. I cannot do it of myself, for I am a poor, weak creature, and Satan knows that if I trust in my own resolution, I shall assuredly fall into his clutches. But I can do all things through Christ who strengtheneth me. O gracious Saviour, save and defend me from my dreadful adversary. Let me lean on Thy arm: let me cling closer to Thee day by day. Grant that I may wish to associate with those who love Thee in sincerity and truth, that I may learn to know myself better, and by talking and thinking more of Thee, may grow daily in grace, and in Thy knowledge and love.

" *Sunday, 6th.*— .... Went to Mr Molyneux's church in the evening, and heard a good sermon, though I was unable duly to appreciate it, as I felt very sleepy. I struggled hard against it, but I lost several sentences. This is because I allow myself to go to sleep after mess every evening, which I must for the future try to prevent."

" *Sunday, 13th.*—Bruce, Dickson, and De Havilland, dined in my room, and we went in the evening to Mr Molyneux's, and heard a most excellent sermon. The text was Ezek. xv. 2, which verse he compared with John xv., and contrasted the two as representing true and nominal believers, and carried out the parallel to shew the utter waste and misery of that represented by Ezekiel, and the worth and beauty of the other described by St John. O heavenly Father, of Thine infinite mercy grant that my case may be represented by St John ; that I be not found a dead and worthless branch, only fit to be cast into everlasting fire. Oh, no, my beloved Saviour ! graft me firmly, truly, and for ever into Thyself, that I may be a living branch, depending solely upon Thee for life and support, and living closer to Thee day by day, that when Thou comest clothed in Thine awful majesty, I may be found, not having my own righteousness, which is but filthy rags, but having the righteousness of God by faith in Thee.

" 14*th*.—In the evening went to ——'s room to play a game of chess. A game of cards was proposed, about which (though I did not join in it myself) I acted very wrongly, in not endeavouring with all my might to prevent its taking place, whereby I injured the yet tender conscience of poor ——. Pardon me, O God, for I have sinned against Thee. Pardon me for Jesus Christ's sake, and enable me to watch better my deceitful heart for the future."

" 22*nd*.—Bruce breakfasted with me. At twelve o'clock went down and played a game at rackets, and afterwards went to the gymnasium. This evening I have had a commune with my own heart about my life, and the way in which I spend my time, and I have come to the conclusion that it is inconsistent with my Christian profession to frequent the billiard-room : therefore it must bo given up, for what saith the Scripture : ' Mortify therefore all your evil and corrupt affections.' Strengthen me by Thy Holy Spirit that I may adhere steadfastly to this resolution ; come and fill my whole heart with love to Thee, and I shall sing of and praise Thine infinite mercy to all eternity.

" 23*rd*.—Played some games of rackets with Bruce, and got beaten, which put my temper to a severe test. And yet why should I care for these trifling things? I want more of Thy grace, holy Saviour, more of Thy

Holy Spirit to raise my thoughts and affections above these passing things."

" 26*th*.—Went after mess to the Artillery Institution, and saw various instruments, and learned the method of making several calculations relative to the weather. Read part of the life of Captain Gordon out of 'The Church in the Army.' The comparison ought to humble me in the dust. Still the old man of sin cleaves to my poor soul, and makes me think too much of the things of the world. Oh, gracious Father, may I always look upon them and the pleasures of sense, as things which perish in the using; and may I ever be mindful that the joys of the world to come will last through all eternity. Keep this continually before my eyes; withdraw my affections from things temporal, and fix them entirely on Thyself. Quicken my faith, pardon my lukewarmness, and strengthen my courage, that I may be able to look every one in the face, feeling a consciousness that I have peace with Thee, through Jesus Christ my Lord. Amen.

" 27*th*.—O God, my humble prayer to Thee is, that Thou wouldst open my lips that my mouth may shew forth Thy praise; that Thou wouldst endue me with powers of persuasion and eloquence, that I may speak of all the wondrous things that Thou hast done for my soul; that I may not blush to own Thy cause, but rather that I may glory in it, for Christ my Saviour's sake. Amen."

"*March* 1*st.*—Went to London to-day to be presented to Prince Albert, but when I got to the palace I felt very unwell, and the crowd was so oppressive, that I was obliged to come away without being presented. Came back to Woolwich, and had the surgeon to see me. It is an attack of fever.

"*2nd.*—Heard very bad news indeed of poor little ——, that he had forsaken the cause of Christ, and had put Him to open shame. Oh, have mercy on him, gracious God! leave him not to the dominion of Satan. Thou who knowest the frailty of the human heart, look not upon him in Thine anger, but grant him Thy Holy Spirit and of Thy infinite mercy bring him back to Thy fold. May it be a warning to me to keep close to the holy Saviour; and do Thou watch over me with a shepherd's care, and let me never wander from Thy side. Give me more, oh, much more of Thy Holy Spirit, to enable me effectually to resist the subtle devices of Satan, and his too willing coadjutor the flesh. For Thine own sake. Amen."

"*8th.*—My beloved Saviour, bring me into closer communion with Thyself. I feel my many infirmities, but with Thee is the well-spring of life; oh, give me out of Thy fulness. Lord, I am faint for want of spiritual food, satisfy the cravings of my hunger, then shall I praise Thee with joyful lips."

"*21st.*—Went out riding with Oldershaw. Visited the Repository, and saw the method of raising a sca-

mortar out of its bed by means of a pair of shears, and
of working guns on traversing platforms."

During these months at Woolwich, Arthur Vandeleur gained the friendship of Colonel, now General
Anderson ; for which, from the date of its commencement until the day of his death, he gave thanks to
God.   In this friendship there was an element of
fatherly love and wisdom, which proved of inestimable
value, not to Arthur only, but also to many other
young officers under Colonel Anderson's command,
who availed themselves of his frank and friendly kindness.   It was offered to all who were within his reach ;
and to how many that Christian and fatherly influence has been made the means of the beginning of a
new life, or of the stablishing, strengthening, and
settling of that life already begun, will never be known
until the day when it shall be revealed how much of
the living water has been permitted to flow through
human channels.

The atmosphere of genial piety in Colonel Anderson's house was rendered yet more delightful to these
young men, by the ready extension of a true motherly
affection and regard, and a kindness which never set a
limit to itself, on the part of Mrs Anderson.

Arthur Vandeleur's charming manners and disposition made him, from the first, a special favourite with
these valued friends; whilst his orphaned heart, always

yearning for affection peculiarly rejoiced in the home thus thrown open to him.

With reference to this period, General Anderson writes :—

"Arthur Vandeleur joined the field batteries of the Royal Artillery under my command as a subaltern, and was an entire stranger to me; but I was, from the first of my intercourse with him, struck by his manly and gentlemanlike bearing, and polished and refined manners.

"I soon found that he possessed all the elements of a thorough soldier. He evinced the greatest possible zeal, smartness, and activity in the discharge of his duty; and, as I was led to believe that he was influenced by Christian principle, although not fully developed, I felt my heart all the more drawn out towards him, and I soon formed a warm affection for him."

On one evening in the week it was Colonel Anderson's custom to open his house to any officers who were willing to partake of his hospitality, and to join in the study of the Holy Scriptures, and in prayer. At these meetings Arthur's bright presence was ever warmly welcomed. And we find in his journal many notices similar to the following of the profit and pleasure he derived from this intercourse :—

"*February* 11*th.*—Went to Colonel Anderson's to breakfast. I like and value him very much indeed:

he is a truly Christian man, and leads a most exemplary life.

"12*th*.—Teach me to recognise and trace Thy Fatherly hand, O my God, in everything that occurs. I see this particularly in the friendship which I have been permitted to form with Colonel Anderson. Oh, may his example and precept stimulate me by Thy assisting grace, to walk more consistently in my profession, and to serve Thee with my whole heart. Enable me to converse and commune more with Thee both in public and in private. Let me delight to talk about Thee; and, whatever I do, in word or deed, may I do all to Thy glory, for my Saviour's sake. Amen."

"15*th*.—After mess, went to Colonel Anderson's, and spent a most pleasant evening. Glory be to God for permitting me to join in prayer and praise with those who really love Him. We read Acts x., and conversed a good deal over it."

Thus did the watchful care of his God and Father provide for the fostering of the heavenly flame, so early kindled in his soul, even in the midst of those floods of temptation incident to the first entrance upon a military life. But the faithful ministry of the gospel, and the holy example and advice of Christian friends, would have availed him little, had he not, by the grace of God, steadfastly and prayerfully set himself to gain, through these means, all the spiritual blessing which they were intended to impart.

With Arthur Vandeleur, religion was not a mere occasional emotion, but an abiding principle. Nor was it a subject only for one half-hour in a day, or one day in a week; but rather was it the first pursuit of his life to become conformed, as far as he perceived it, to the will of his God. Although he had not yet attained to the full knowledge that the peace which passeth all understanding was so left by the Redeemer of the world, as to be claimed by all who believe in Him, as their immediate and abiding portion; still he was one of those to whom the promise could not fail to be fulfilled: "Then shall they know, if they follow on to know the Lord."

And whilst he had not yet entered upon "the glorious liberty of the children of God," he was doing battle manfully against the enslaving forces of sin and Satan. And those who lovingly watched and aided his progress, foresaw that the end of these upward strivings of his earnest spirit, in God's good time would be, the emerging from every mist into the bright and holy calm of a conscious fellowship with the Father, and with His Son Jesus Christ.

Excepting in times when the very windows of heaven are opened for the pouring out of blessings; "times of refreshing from the presence of the Lord," cases of sudden conversion have been comparatively rare. The more frequent manner of God's dealing with the heart of man, in common seasons, seems to correspond with its type, as given in Holy Writ, of the gradual development of the seed which has been sown in the earth; in taking root, then springing up—"first the blade, then the ear, after that, the full corn in the ear."

But not because we trace in the lovely life of Arthur Vandeleur, the rich harvest which was raised by the Divine husbandman through rainy days and stormy winds, and days of warm sunshine and balmy breezes, would we depreciate the glorious work of the Holy Spirit in a sudden and abiding conversion. God forbid we should limit Him to our slow ideas of progress; or hinder Him from "doing many mighty works amongst us, because of our unbelief."

In the sacred story of the early days of a triumphant gospel, have we not repeated records of instantaneous conversions?

Zaccheus, the chief of a class who amassed their fortunes by fraud or violence, hears the voice of an unknown Saviour saying to him, "To-day I must abide at thy house." He makes haste, and receives Him joyfully; and is transformed into a just and a generous man, by that ennobling Presence. "Behold, Lord,"—behold what Thou hast wrought in one brief hour—"the half of my goods I give to the poor : and if I have taken anything from any man by false accusation, I restore him fourfold."

A sinful woman of Samaria hears the Divine voice of a wearied Stranger, resting on a well, saying, " If thou wouldst have asked, He would have given thee living water." " Whosoever drinketh of the water that I shall give him, shall never thirst ; but the water that I shall give him shall be in him a well of water, springing up into everlasting life ; " and from the draught of that pure water given her in her communing with a holy Saviour, the unholy one goes forth, with purity and peace in her bosom, to become a preacher of Jesus to her fellow-sinners. " COME, SEE A MAN who told me all things that ever I did ;—IS NOT THIS THE CHRIST ? And many believed on Him for the saying of the woman."

A Saul of Tarsus goes forth from Jerusalem to Damascus, " exceeding mad against the faith ; " " breathing out threatenings and slaughter against the disciples of the Lord ; " and suddenly, at mid-day, there shines about him a light from heaven, above the brightness of the sun ; and as he falls to the earth, he hears the voice of Him who saith to His people, " Whoso toucheth you, toucheth the apple of mine eye," asking " O thou sought out, O thou sought out,* why persecutest thou Me ? " And meekly, out of the depths of a broken and a contrite heart, Saul replies, in words which condense into their brief compass the fealty

* English rendering of the name of " Saul."

of the servant with the duty of the son, "Lord, what wilt Thou have me to do?"

Ananias is sent at once, to call the great persecutor of the day a "brother;" for he is a chosen vessel unto the Lord, to suffer, in his turn, great things for His name's sake; and to bear His name before the Gentiles, and kings, and the children of Israel.—And he is to be sent unto them "NOW;" "to open their eyes, and to turn them from darkness to light, and from the power of Satan unto God."

Three thousand men, whose hands were red with the blood of the innocent Lamb of God—three thousand of those from whose crime the very sun had turned away, shutting out its glories from a world which had consented to the murder of its anointed King—were pricked to the heart at one moment under the preaching of Peter; and they, too, at once received remission of sins and the gift of the Holy Ghost, with their open confession of faith in a crucified Saviour, and the outward seal of the covenant.

"And they continued *steadfastly* in the apostles' doctrine and fellowship, and in breaking of bread, and in prayers."

CHAPTER V.

True Heroism.

" Promptness to aid in one another's needs,
With self-denial, yea, heroic acts,
The more heroic, as not knowing themselves
For such at all."

In the autumn of the year 1848, Arthur Vandeleur was promoted to be first lieutenant;[*] and was posted to a company in Jamaica.

Unfortunately no letters written by him at this time have been preserved; but one who well remembers having read many which he then wrote to her father and brothers, recalls, with no slight regret for their loss, their manly and spirited tone, and vivid descriptions of the beautiful scenery of the island, with the tropical brilliancy of its colouring, and of its gorgeous birds and flowers. He had purchased a pleasure-boat at this time, and greatly delighted in sailing expeditions with his brother officers at Port-Royal. Their favourite amusement was the pursuit of the devil-fish; and many an exciting race out to sea they had after these creatures. At this period of his life, Arthur's daring was scarcely tempered by "the better part of valour;" and he not unfrequently found himself in considerable danger in the midst of sudden squalls on

[*] At that time, there were *first* and *second* lieutenants in the Royal Artillery.

the somewhat impracticable coast of the island. But his frequent escapes from perilous adventures rather added to the charm of putting to sea again for fresh chases in doubtful weather, unsuited to his frail little yacht, and his exulting spirits ever rose with the breezes, and the tossing of the sea.

This little yacht of his was destined to a noble purpose before he left the island, as we find recorded in a letter from General Armstrong, R.A., to General Anderson. Whilst Arthur Vandeleur was under Colonel Armstrong's command in Jamaica, in the month of October, 1850, Asiatic cholera suddenly broke out in the garrison, and seventeen persons died of it in the course of a few hours. Immediate burial was necessary to save the rest of the garrison. The burial-place was a considerable distance off, along the coast, and the land-way to it lay through very deep sand. In consequence of this, funeral-parties always went thither by water; but at this time the panic was so great, that no boats could be procured at any price for the purpose of conveying the bodies of those who had died of cholera. In this emergency, Arthur Vandeleur came forward at once with the offer of his pleasure-boat; and, with the aid of one man, who volunteered his assistance, he carried the dead on board, and conveyed them to their last earthly resting-place.

We learn from General Armstrong's letter that, but for this heroic effort, they must have remained unburied, and that terribly fatal might have been the consequences to the remainder of the garrison. Shortly afterwards, Arthur was himself seized with cholera, and was brought down to the very gate of death. But, by God's blessing on the remedies applied by loving hands—for he was nursed by his servant with devoted attachment—he was spared for ten years more of usefulness in his Master's service, and of making happy, with no common happiness, those who were privileged to enjoy intimate intercourse with him.

One of the married soldiers and his wife died in one day, of this visitation of cholera. And the wife's sister still tells with overflowing gratitude how Mr Vandeleur cared for them in their short illness; and that, when they were dead, he took their little orphaned babe, and kept it, and fed it, until he had found a trusty nurse, whom he engaged to take care of it; nor even then ceased to watch over his little charge. "Oh," said the poor woman, as she told the story, "he was a loving-hearted gentleman! You should hear the black people talk of him, and of all his goodness to them!"

Whilst he was in Jamaica, he obtained the valuable friendship of the Rev. V. J. P. Donet, Rector of St Elizabeth's, Annetto Bay; for whom, as well as for Mrs Donet, he ever retained a grateful and affectionate regard.

His bright cheerfulness and ready good nature made

him a great favourite with the children at the Rectory, and two of them used to write to him occasionally after his return to England.

Mr Donet thus speaks of the period of his acquaintance with him:—

" . . . . Mrs Donet and myself formed a very great attachment for him, as he completely became one of us during his sojourn of six weeks in our family. . . . We first met him at Port-Royal, at the house of my brother-in-law, Mr Hale, the late Rector, where he always spent his Sabbath afternoons, so as to be quiet with him, away from the bustle of the garrison, and to be ready for the evening service. On our leaving, we asked him to come down to St Elizabeth's; which he did, and was so happy, that he applied for a renewal of leave, and spent six weeks with us instead of three, as at first proposed. I have every reason to believe that this was made a time of blessing to him, as he frequently said how much good he had derived from his visit, especially in regard to separation from the world. He had ever found it difficult to draw the line, as to how far he should mix up with it, and enjoy its pleasures; but he said, the evening before he left, 'I have to thank God from my heart that I came here, I see now the path of duty more clearly than I have ever done before; and, through God's grace, I have resolved, cost what it may, to 'come out, and be separate.'

"We devoted every morning to religious conversation and reading the Scriptures; he questioning me on several difficult passages, and sitting as a disciple to be instructed in the things of God; and I assure you it was pleasant to see how *greedily* he received the Word. Often have I seen him melted to tears, when I have related some striking anecdote which at one time or another had occurred during my ministry. But one especially affected him. It was of a dying man, who, when his medical adviser told him that he had not an hour to live, exclaimed, 'I cannot die—I cannot stand before an angry God.'

"This had a great effect on him, and as he occupied the room immediately under mine, I could hear him during the former part of the night, agonising with God in prayer. My wife had an equally deep affection for him with my own; and she and I have often regretted that we had not a more frequent correspondence with our truly valued friend."

He did not remain long in Jamaica after this visit, only a few weeks, as the cholera broke out among the troops, and they were removed away as early as possible.

With reference to that time, we have this additional testimony, in a letter dated November 29, 1861, from General Armstrong, for whom Arthur ever retained a most grateful regard:—

". . . . . The cholera broke out amongst us in September 1850, and carried off about one-third of our little garrison at Port-Royal within a month. Nothing could exceed the unwearied attention, affectionate kindness, and moral courage displayed by poor dear Vandeleur during his voluntary attendance upon the sick and the dying, until the disease attacked him, amongst the last of the sufferers, and he very nearly fell a victim to it.

"His whole life, ever since I have known him, in Jamaica and elsewhere, was always that of a kind, noble-hearted, truly Christian gentleman.

"He was beloved by me nearly as a son, on account of his numerous virtues and many endearing qualities, and his death I most sincerely and deeply deplore."

CHAPTER VI.

The Light Burning.

"Lord, in the strength of grace,
With a glad heart and free,
Myself, my residue of days,
I consecrate to Thee."

E

Arthur Vandeleur's kind and thoughtful guardian was anxious that his ward should return for his coming of age, on the 21st of January, 1850 ; in order that the attachment between himself and his tenantry might have the additional tie of this eventful day being spent amongst them, with the usual rejoicings on such an occasion. But Arthur found that it would be undesirable to press for his leave, before the return of his company ; which did not take place until the month of February, 1851.

Immediately on his arrival, as he was now in his twenty-third year, he undertook the management of his own affairs, the prosperous state of which he owed to the wise and generous care of his deeply-valued guardian, Mr Molony.

One of his first desires was to atone, as far as it was possible, for the heavy losses his father had occasioned to several persons, in various positions of life, by failures in wild speculations. And although they had no legal claim upon the son for the debts of the father, Arthur Vandeleur borrowed a large sum of money on mortgage of the estate, in order to make repayment as far as possible; thereby not a little impoverishing himself for the rest of his life.

On his return to Woolwich, he resumed his old and beloved position of a son with a father, towards Colonel Anderson. In his diary, which was either not written, or not preserved, during his residence in Jamaica, but which was now resumed and kept with great regularity, we find frequent records of the happy evenings spent at "his colonel's" house; and of the portions of Scripture which were read and discussed there.

His mind was developing itself rapidly at this time; and the natural love of reading which he had shewn in his boyish days, now led him to devote a good deal of his leisure time to study. The cast of his mind caused him chiefly to choose those books which required reflection; and which tended to increase and strengthen his mental powers. He was not satisfied, with reading merely in a desultory manner, to pass the time pleasantly; but he exercised a considerable amount of determination and self-control, in turning this reading to the best account. This appears in the following rules which are worthy of notice, especially as having been framed, and, for the most part, rigidly observed, by so young a man; although they may have been rather too stringent to allow free play to his intellect.

Remarks.

"Having found that I do not remember for any considerable length of time what I have read, and knowing that memory consists, to a great extent, in attention, I conclude that I do not read with attention. To make myself do so, I propose the following plan, which, though undoubtedly a slow one, is, I think, a *sure* one; for, as the victorious tortoise said to the hare,—

'Slow and steady wins the race.'

"My plan is this—

"1st, To write down all the principal ideas and sentiments, &c., of every book which I may read, as concisely as possible, in my own words.

"2nd, To write each day what I have read on the previous day.

"3rd, On Saturday to read only religious works—that I may be able to write on Sunday what I have read on the previous day, without *transgressing the commands* of my good God and Saviour. Reading these works alone, on Saturday, (not on Saturday *only*,) will tend to prepare my mind for closer communion with my holy Father on His own day.

"4th, To suffer nothing to interfere with this writing. Should duty or disinclination prevent me from keeping this rule, *resolved* to read nothing (save one newspaper) but God's Holy Word and the little commentary, until I have performed this duty, though the condemnation should last some days; except under unusual circumstances, such as a journey.

" 5th, Should I fail to remember (without referring to the book) what I have read, *resolved* to recommence reading at the place of failure, till I can express the author's meaning properly.

" 6th, To make what remarks I can on the subject treated of, so as to accustom myself both to reflect on what I read, and to express, in suitable language, my ideas.

" 7th, To commence reading in this manner to-day. Oh, Almighty God, Thou who knowest how impossible it is for man either to think a good thought of himself, or to act aright in his own strength, as it is Thou who hast put the wish into my heart to improve my mind for Thy service, do Thou give me energy and determination, that I may persevere in doing my best, to Thy glory."

" *Saturday, September 6th.*—Played chess in the evening with De Havilland. We are a good match; but my wretched pride, whenever I am beaten, tries to make me deny the superiority of his play to mine during that game. Oh, my God, humble me, overcome this horrid pride in me, for Jesus' sake. Amen."

" *Saturday, September 13th.*—Rose very late this morning. This is very bad. Seven hours' sleep is as much as I require; so, if I go to bed at eleven, I ought to get up at six; but I am so lazy and slothful, that I seldom get up till my servant has called me two or three times. I fear that in this, as in other ways, I may dishonour my Christian profession. O Lord, teach me to overcome it. Give me grace and strength to do so. Now, Lord, I will make a new start; to-morrow I will try to rise at six, and, for the future, will always try and get to bed at eleven. Read little to-day. Evident sign that I rose too late. Whenever I do that, the day slips through my fingers before I can do anything."

" *Tuesday, September* 16*th.*—Dined with dear Colonel Anderson. Mr Yorke and many Christian friends came in the evening. Colonel Anderson requested me to pray; but oh, because I was filled with self, I was so nervous that I could hardly express an idea. Oh, subdue self and pride, wretched pride, my Saviour, and fill me with Thyself, Thy gracious self. Give me the power of expressing my thoughts, for Jesus' sake. Amen."

" *September* 18*th.*—Read a good deal of Young's ' Night Thoughts' in the omnibus. The thoughts are deep; but the subject, ' The Glory of God, as shewn by the Stars and the Heavens,' causes it to be unusually fine, even for him. Felt my mind benefited by it, and my thoughts kept from wandering in forbidden and unhallowed regions. For this I praise Thee, my ·Father, through Jesus Christ. Determine, in consequence, frequently to take this book with me."

"*Sabbath-day, September 21st.*—Dr Duff, the celebrated Scotch missionary from India, preached, and I thank God that I heard him. His text was Psalm cxxx. 3, 4. "If Thou, Lord, shouldst mark iniquities, O Lord, who shall stand? But there is forgiveness with Thee, that Thou mayest be feared." Through the mercy of my Saviour, I have derived much benefit from Dr Duff, and I trust, from this time forth, to take an active interest in the evangelisation of the poor heathen. I must begin at once, and will do so. Oh, my God, do Thou cleanse my heart in the blood of Thy dear Son. Now that I here give Thee my heart, surely the outworks will all become Thine. Yes, Lord, I devote myself, my life, my all, to Thy service. What wouldst Thou have me to do? I implore of Thee, the living God, never to leave me, but to perfect Thine own work, and to make me altogether like my glorious Lord and Master; and oh, was not He holy and humble? Oh, make me holy and humble for His sake. Amen."

The dangerous amusement of billiard-playing, for a short time, again became a snare to him. Games of hazard, like deeds of adventure, could not fail to have an ensnaring fascination for such a character as his. But when he heard that his mere appearance at the public billiard-table brought a reproach upon the name of his Lord, and did an injury to the souls of some who were keenly watching the consistency of his Christian example, he renounced the long-questioned amusement at once and for ever, for the honour of his Master, and for the sake of immortal souls, "for whom Christ died;" in the spirit of the great heart of an Apostle, who said, "I will eat no meat while the world standeth, if it cause my brother to offend."

Arthur was now fast losing all sense of the need of exciting pleasures, for he was daily discovering more and more of that "kingdom of God," into which he had entered, and which is "righteousness, and peace, and joy in the Holy Ghost." In grasping more firmly the higher pleasures, the lower fled away, and were desired no more. And in the new interest of winning souls to Jesus, he found a deeper stake and a more glorious gain than aught that he had dreamt of before.

A few more short extracts from his journal will give an idea of the conscientious watch which he maintained, at this time, over his progress in the spiritual life :—

" *September* 30th.—On looking back over this month, I find that I have much reason to thank and praise my God for giving me perseverance to continue to keep my journal, which helps me to hold communion with Him; and also for enabling me to be more careful of my time during the past month; and for keeping me from the billiard-room and racket-court, where my energies used to be exhausted and my mind (too often) corrupted. I give my God hearty thanks for His help granted me to resign these ensnaring amusements; but much more for the insight He has given me into the evil of my own heart, and for leading me to flee to Christ for salvation. ALL my hope is in Jesus Christ, my Lord and Master. Truly, His yoke is easy, and His burden is light. And I pray, by His might in the inner man, to be enabled to withstand Satan, *self*, and sin.

"*October 9th.*—— —— arrived from Jamaica, and came to see me. He was not fortunate or happy there, and is now very ill with rheumatic gout. He stayed with me for sometime, and I was enabled by God's grace to speak seriously to him, and gently (I hope) to shew him how foolish his former conduct had been. I was also helped to bear my small testimony to the happiness which is to be found in Jesus, if we place all our dependence upon Him, and determine with *all our heart* to serve Him. I pray and trust that the Lord will lead him to Himself."

"*October 12th.*—Had a pleasant day at the Sunday-school. My boys are getting on pretty well. I was helped to speak to them earnestly and affectionately. Oh, may the word take root in their little hearts, that they may be brought to know and love their Saviour."

At this time, Arthur was making frequent visits to the Great Exhibition in Hyde Park; and both taking sketches, and writing copious notes in his diary, describing the various models of machinery, and representations of scientific discoveries and improvements. In such details he was always remarkably correct and clear. He took great delight in these visits, and also in spending leisure hours in various picture galleries. Yet in the midst of these pleasurable engagements, we find him not unmindful of his Master's work.

"*October* 18*th*.—Went with P—— to Dulwich Picture Gallery to-day. Had a very pleasant ride; but did not speak of the things of God to him, so earnestly as I ought to have done. Ah, how often does a casual and cold observation compose the sum-total of my exertions in the cause of Christ. Pardon, oh pardon, my miserable selfishness, blessed Saviour. How can I, upon whom Thou hast bestowed Thy mercy and Thy Love, be ashamed of speaking of Thee; or at least, if not ashamed, wanting in patience and in persevering energy, to bear the first adverse remark with meekness, and at the same time to continue my purpose. I feel sure that if I did this, Thou wouldst bless the effort. Give me more faith and more grace and courage, gracious Saviour."

With reference to this time, Colonel Anderson writes: "Arthur Vandeleur was for some months under my immediate command; and as my valued friend, Sir Hew Ross, the Adjutant-General of the Artillery, was

in the habit of frequently interrogating me with regard
to the character of the young officers under my charge,
I had peculiar pleasure in pointing out Vandeleur as
one in every way deserving of his approbation; and he
was pleased, at my recommendation, to note his name
for the Horse Artillery, to which branch of the service,
he was shortly afterwards appointed; and joined Captain
Maude's troop in Ireland."

CHAPTER VII.

Earnest Working.

"Yes! He is mine! And nought of earthly things,
Not all the charms of pleasure, wealth, or power,
The fame of heroes, or the pomp of kings,
Could tempt me to forego His love an hour:
'Go, worthless world,' I cry, 'with all that 's thine!
Go! I my Saviour's am, and He is mine.'

"The good I have is from His stores supplied;
The ill is only what He deems the best:
He for my Friend, I 'm rich with nought beside,
And poor without Him, though of all possess'd.
Changes may come, I take, or I resign,
Content while I am His, while He is mine!"

THE two years spent in Dublin by Arthur Vandeleur, appear to have been a delightful time of refreshing to his own soul, and to those with whom he held chief intercourse. Nor did he feel it necessary now to confine himself to efforts to win his personal friends and acquaintance to the knowledge and love of that Saviour who was every day manifesting Himself more fully to his soul, as the "altogether lovely One;" nor to set as boundaries to his zeal, the gates of the barrack-yard. But whilst the soldier, and the gunner especially amongst soldiers, ever claimed his deepest interest and his most loving effort, Arthur's large heart embraced in its desires the spiritual welfare of all his fellow-creatures in the lost world, which has been redeemed by the blood of Christ. And remembering the example of his Lord, who came to call *sinners* to repentance, and who told the depth and the breadth of His love in the brief sentence, "The Son of Man is come to seek and to save that which is *lost ;*" he set himself earnestly, prayerfully, and lovingly to work amongst the outcast population of the "St Giles's" of Dublin.

Finding how necessary were combination and system, to extensive success in so wide a field, he united with great ardour in assisting in the formation of a large Ragged School in one of the poorest and wildest districts in Dublin; and himself undertook to be its superintendent.

"His task there," writes the Rev. C. W. Fleury,* "was a difficult one at first; when a multitude of uninstructed creatures were assembled from Sunday to Sunday—ignorant of all religion save the worst form of Romanism; destitute of all respect for every one superior in education and position; and habituated from infancy to every grossness of language and manners. These assemblies numbered amongst them some of the vilest characters; and to their depredations he was constantly exposed; having often to recount to us his losses of money, trinkets, and handkerchiefs, which were purloined during the exercise of his arduous office."

But his undaunted heart never failed him; cheered on by Christian hope and faith, his patient persevering love worked wonders with those uncivilised creatures, rarely leaving any as he found them; and to many, his instructions were a source of thanksgiving for both this life and the next. His removal from Dublin was to them a source of the most genuine and bitter sorrow.

* Incumbent of the Molyneux Episcopal Chapel.

The dear and valued friend of Arthur Vandeleur, to whom we owe these details, bears the following testimony to his character during his stay in Dublin :—

"Our intimacy grew out of spiritual things. He was a member of my congregation in the Molyneux Asylum Chapel; and our friendship ripened, as I became gradually acquainted with the high qualities with which he was endowed. He was a diligent and animated attendant at regular evening meetings held in my house; which were arranged with a view to win literary men to take an interest in religion. Our recreation consisted generally, in the early part of the evening, in reading original and well-selected papers and passages, and subsequently in studying critically and prayerfully an appointed portion of Scripture.

"Our young friend, Mr S——, who was one of the regular attendants at these meetings, we watched with much anxiety, as he possessed great amiability, and had what would be termed deep convictions, but confessed with great candour, and deplored with much bitterness, his frailties and infirmity of better purpose. He was subject to epilepsy, under an attack of which he suddenly died. To him, poor fellow, Arthur was an object of the utmost wonder, as well as a friend for whom he entertained the most profound respect.

"The cheerfulness, manliness, steady piety, and unostentatious zeal for all good things which Arthur exhibited, added to his well-known virtues as a son and relative, gave him a degree of weight and dignity which overwhelmed every small opposition to his pure religion, which might naturally spring up in the mind of an unconverted stranger on first meeting him.

"Hence, amongst his brother-officers at Portobello Barracks, as well as amongst the soldiers who passed under his care, there was ever exhibited towards him the most unconditional respect.

"Twice every Sunday he attended the services in my church, notwithstanding his arduous labours at the Ragged School.

"At our evening meetings, which he heartily enjoyed, we frequently entered into the study of unfulfilled prophecy. And when rumours of a war in the East became strong and decisive, he was much interested in the views we entertained; and he endeavoured to prove from Ezekiel xxxvii. and xxxviii., that the war, then on the eve of commencement, was *not* the final war in which the Czar of Russia was to take so prominent a part, and which is reserved for the period immediately succeeding the approaching restoration of the Jews to the Holy Land. He therefore conjectured that the war which then required his removal from home, would be but short, and that, by God's good Providence, he might soon be meeting his friends in Ireland and England again!

"God did spare him for that meeting again! And we had the joy of receiving him under our roof soon after his return home, prior to his entering on the duties of his appointment at Woolwich. A joy which was not marred by any apprehension that his removal to another world was drawing near ; for he was then, apparently, in the highest health as well as spirits.

"His noble character and wonderful amiability, all under the controlling influence of his genuine Christian piety, have left an impression for good on the minds and hearts of all who knew him. In fact, whilst we fondly look back upon our intimacy with him as one of the brightest spots in our lives' history, we rejoice to know that the same happy and hallowed influence accompanied him wherever he went."

Arthur Vandeleur found a second home in Dublin, in the house of Mr Despard, whose friendship he esteemed as a peculiar gift, when he was quartered in a gay capital, where there was much to tempt him into frivolous and unprofitable amusements. He frequently left the mess-table to spend his evenings in the society of his friend. "His delight," writes Mr Despard, " was to converse about his Master's kingdom and its interests ; and never have I known any Christian to whom mere worldly topics of conversation were so distasteful ; or who had a happier method of bringing other minds to centre on what was the grand subject of thought with his own mind.

" His Sundays at that time were nearly always spent with us. Every Sabbath afternoon we used to go down together to a Ragged School consisting chiefly of adult Roman Catholics, in one of the most degraded districts of Dublin. His earnest anxiety to find an avenue of approach to the ignorant and superstitious minds of the poor, miserable-looking creatures who formed his class; and his warm-hearted, affectionate addresses to the whole assembly at the close of the school, (of which he was superintendent,) will long be remembered by those who were so favoured as to be able to observe and to hear them. It was indeed a privilege, for the couple of years that he was quartered in Dublin, to be an eye-witness of his consistent and devoted Christian life."

An index to his mind and to his motives of action, at this time, is given in the following letters :—

"R. A. BARRACKS, PORTOBELLO,
"*August 1st*, 1853.

"MY DEAR BRUCE,— . . . . I have had so much official correspondence to carry on, that I have for some time neglected nearly all my friends. However, I trust that this is now at an end, and hope to be more regular for the future in replying to your kind and welcome letters. It was indeed a disappointment to know that you could not pay your promised visit to me this year, but I hope you will come before I leave Ireland, that we may have the pleasure of going together to see some of its numerous, though somewhat scattered beauties. Speaking on this subject, where do you think I have been playing the truant to? No less a place than the far-famed Killarney. It came to pass in this way: I had to go down to Clare to record my vote at the late election for Colonel Vandeleur, and to bring a few of my '*tinants*' with me to the poll, so, having to get leave from the General for that purpose, I got a few extra days, and went to Killarney. Its beautiful scenery charmed me very much; but, being quite alone, I found it rather solitary work, and much wished to have you with me. You must really come over to Old Ireland, if it were only to see that one charming spot. Much as I had heard of its beauties, I was not in the least disappointed, but rather the reverse. It is just the place you would delight in, being well calculated to store your mind with poetic ideas, having, within the compass of twenty miles, every species of beautiful scenery, and not an ugly or uninteresting spot in it all—mountains craggy and bare, with magnificent precipices and bold outlines, and with very fine echoes, many times repeated. Then, within a short distance, mountains with gentle, undulating slopes, clad to the very summit with oak, fir, and arbutus trees. You have also various waterfalls and rapids, rivers and lakes of all shapes and sizes, old abbeys and modern churches, ruined castles situated on islands and peninsulas, and modern ones, their rivals in beauty and elegance, if not in age. But it is a place of which description would fail to give you any adequate idea; therefore, I say, you must come over when you can, and see and judge for yourself, and if you will make me your travelling companion, I shall be truly rejoiced, dear Bruce. I could only remain there three days when on leave; but it is a place which affords points of interest for a much longer time, had one but the leisure. But enough of Killarney for the present. You will be glad to know that I continue to like Dublin very much. I think it one of our best stations. It has many spiritual advantages. I do not now attend the controversial lectures, not because I feel less interest in them than formerly, but because I really have not time to do so. Our Ragged School is progressing favourably; it is a very valuable institution, and is the means of doing much good. My class of old women continues to interest me as much as ever. I have some who are very regular attendants, and who appear to take an interest in what they hear; indeed, I trust the Lord has touched the hearts of some of them. This is to me a matter of deep thankfulness to Almighty God; may all the glory and praise be to His most holy name. Oh, dear Bruce, it would delight you to see the eyes of these poor creatures, taken from amongst the lowest of the Irish paupers, sparkle with delight, and their miserable, haggard countenances grow happy, for the time, when they are told of the love of Jesus. You can imagine what encouragement these little circumstances give me. I sometimes feel as if one such were sufficient reward for a year's labour. The priests hate us most cordially, and curse any one who will come to our school; still they come, and our numbers increase. So much for the priests' influence in Dublin. Would to God they had no more elsewhere! but it is being undermined, I trust and think, everywhere. It afforded me pleasure and happiness of the most intense kind, to learn from your ownself of your temporal and spiritual welfare, and that Jesus is becoming every day more precious to your soul. Praised be His holy name for His great mercies to you. Indeed, Bruce, since I last wrote, I too have received signal mercies at the hand of God, for which, I think, I am not ungrateful. I trust, also, that I have progressed somewhat on my road Heavenward; but not so much as I might have done. Oh, how I long to see you, and converse with you. . . . . I hope that we shall yet be quartered together—the sooner the better. Meantime, let us pray for each other more earnestly than ever. I send you a little paper given me by a valued friend a few days since. It will, I hope, stir you up to oppose the Man of sin, even more than you have yet done. Tell me what you think of it, in your next. W——, whom you well know, is my chief here; he is very kind to me and all of us, and is very much liked; but for the sake of my profession, I could wish that he was somewhat more strict and regular. It is good for young fellows to be under *tight hands!* It is just possible that I may go to Chobham and Woolwich in about ten days to get my shot tried, &c. &c.—Your affectionate friend,　　　　　A. V."

TO COLONEL ANDERSON, R.A.

"PORTOBELLO, *August* 18*th*, 1852.

"MY DEAR COLONEL,—Your kind and welcome letter afforded me the greatest pleasure, and I have to thank you in the warmest manner for your kind wishes and advice, which prove that you still continue to remember me. We do indeed require constant exhortation to persevere in the conflict against Satan and indwelling sin, by making diligent use of the means of grace. These are the weapons which are provided for our warfare, and is it not comforting to know that their effect upon our enemies depends, not upon the strength of the arm that uses them, but rather upon the almighty power of the great Captain of our Salvation?

"It requires to be impressed constantly upon the mind, that the work of sanctification has to be performed in us and by us, as fellow-workers with God. We are so prone to think that we have nothing to do but to sit still and wait for our hearts to be renewed. But though it is quite true that we cannot change our own hearts, yet we can lay ourselves under the changing, transforming influences of God's Holy Spirit. Though we cannot turn of ourselves, yet we can frame our doings to turn; and it is for the neglect of this duty that Rehoboam is so much blamed—'He did evil because he prepared not his heart to seek the Lord.'

"The work of reformation is, I hope, still progressing in Ireland; and I fervently pray, that it may never cease till the whole island become 'full of the knowledge of the Lord, as the waters cover the sea.'

"My time is at present well occupied, as besides being in battery, I am doing Quartermaster duty, during the absence of Mr Murray on leave. Captain Fitzgerald has been very ill for some time past; he has suffered great pain, which he bears with truly Christian patience and resignation. When I saw him, four days ago, he was quite unable to move his right arm, and looked very much reduced. It is a pleasure to me to visit him, as I derive benefit from his conversation. I told him that I was going to write to you, and he desired to be most affectionately remembered. . . . . . I shall never cease to remember your kindness to me with the deepest gratitude.—Ever, my dear Colonel very sincerely yours,

" ARTHUR VANDELEUR."

The long residence of Arthur Vandeleur in Dublin, necessarily involved him in a larger circle of acquaintance than he would have met with in other quarters. The singular charm of his manners, and the combination of brilliant personal attractions with a graceful readiness in communicating the resources of a cultivated understanding, could not fail to render him a welcome addition to any society. Every evening might have been spent by him in the pursuit of pleasures which assuredly would not have eluded the grasp of such a votary.

But now that he had wholly surrendered every power and every affection to that Saviour who loved him and gave Himself for him, Arthur arrived at the conclusion, that the great object of life, for a Christian, is not—how much he may enjoy of the pleasures of a world which has not yet crowned his King ; and the spirit of which is so much in opposition to its rightful Sovereign, as to be described in His Word, as "enmity with God;" but rather, how much he may attain of blessed fellowship with his Saviour, and what are the things to be avoided, as endangering the possession of that chief joy.

He was already acting upon the principle of four simple rules, his ready acceptance of which, when conversing on this subject, a few years later, I well remember :—

"Let me never be found where I could not expect to

meet my Saviour, if He were still a man on the earth : where I could not ask Him to be present with me, by His Spirit, now : where I could not be occupied in seeking, as opportunity offered, to win others to Him : or where I should not like Him to find me, when ' coming suddenly.' "

The attraction of mere amusement would now, indeed, have been easily resisted by him. But sometimes, by his young imagination, there was thrown over those scenes of gaiety the same golden glow which the early morning of his heart had shed over different scenes, in a sweet home of the wild country of the west.

It was a trial of his faith, when he felt it to be his duty to avoid seeking out anywhere and everywhere, that gentle companionship, the charm of which had never lessened for his steadfast heart. But he stood the test, "strong in the grace which is in Christ Jesus :" and, shunning the labyrinth of human probabilities and means of success, he trusted the garnered hopes of boyhood and manhood on the venture of an absolute confidence in the power and kindness of that God, who pledges Himself to each of His children still, as surely as He did to the man after His own heart, three thousand years ago—" Delight thyself also in the Lord, and he shall give thee the desires of thine heart."

" Strong faith," said a man of God, " must have strong trials." And the Word of God gives the reason for it : " That the trial of your faith, being much more precious than of gold that perisheth, though it be tried with fire, might be found unto praise and honour and glory, at the appearing of Jesus Christ."

The faith of Arthur Vandeleur was destined to be thus proved. Obstacles, apparently almost insurmountable, stood opposed to the fulfilment of his wishes. But whilst keenly feeling the present trial, he possessed his soul in patience; for in his heart there was a sea of peace, and the current of those troubled waters could only ruffle the surface.

The following letter to his friend Captain Bruce, was written at this time :—

"FASSEROE, CO. WICKLOW,
October 28th, 1852.

"MY DEAR BRUCE,—Amidst severe sorrows, it has been to me a source of much comfort that in you I have a friend upon whose regard and affection I can rely. The day before I received your valued letter, my attention was drawn by one of our brother-officers to that paragraph in your journal which announced the death of poor dear Orme. Though I had no definite reason for disbelieving the statement, still, until I heard direct from you, I did not believe it; because, I suppose, my hopes and wishes were against my doing so.

"It is indeed, my dear Bruce, a heavy blow to both of us; but especially so to you; and I do sympathise most deeply with you. He was to each of us a most valued friend, and to me a kind and able adviser, for he understood more of the workings of my mind than did any other of my friends or acquaintance. I do therefore deeply deplore his loss. How much more must you! for I saw long ago that your minds were so similar, that they almost seemed to have been cast in the same mould. It was no wonder, then, that you should be drawn together in such strong bonds of friendship, almost immediately on coming into contact with each other. I do therefore deeply feel for you, my dear friend, for I know when the string of a powerful bow gives way, how dreadful is the recoil.

"It seems very sad that Orme should have been called away so early when his career of usefulness in his Master's cause was, *to our eyes*, but just begun. And at a time, too, when those who are entirely devoted to the service of God, especially in the army, can but ill be spared. But the Master knows best about it; and we are therefore bound to believe that our dear friend has been called away *just at the proper time*. We know too that he has fulfilled the great end for which he was born;—he has glorified God in his generation. And now he is with, and *like*, his Saviour. *What happiness!* Oh, that the same testimony with regard to us and our conduct may be able with truth to be borne by those who have known us best, when we, likewise, shall be called out of this world of sin and sorrow. Orme was one of those few whose 'whole body was full of light' because 'his eye was single.' What a cold heartless wretch I feel myself to be, when compared with him!

"You will pardon my apparent neglect in not writing to you about this loss, at once; but it arose neither from indifference nor laziness. My heart was overwhelmed with the severity of another affliction, different in kind, but more painful than I could tell you. It occurred a few days after your letter reached me, and so completely occupied my mind that I could give my thoughts to nothing else. However, my dear Bruce, God Himself has comforted my soul, and has given me grace to say from my inmost heart, 'Thy will be done, O my God!'

"He has made me to see His merciful hand even in those things in which at first I could trace only His displeasure. From the 145th hymn in the second volume of Sacred Poetry I have derived great comfort, particularly from verses two and three.

"I am trying to get 'leave' from the 1st of November to travel on the Continent—I think in France and Italy. How I wish you could come. Many reasons combine to make me wish to go at this time; and I am given to understand that I shall be unable to get away after next March. However, if you are going early next year, I will try my best, but am not sanguine about it.

"The only letter I have had lately from Woolwich was from Desborough. He says they are all getting on well. You, I suppose, hear from the dear old Colonel. Ever your affectionate friend,

"ARTHUR VANDELEUR."

In the end of 1852, having obtained leave of absence, he was able to fulfil his desire of spending a short time upon the Continent.

His journey through Paris, Lyons, Marseilles, Genoa, and Florence, to Rome, afforded him many opportunities of satisfying that thirst for knowledge which was, from his childhood, a distinguishing feature of his mind. He found great enjoyment in a careful study of the chief objects of interest in the great towns through which he passed ; and in a long letter to his kind friend Colonel Anderson, he describes minutely the fortifications of Paris and Lyons, which he had opportunities of examining ; and draws a comparison between the advantages of the French and English artillery, in system, dress, &c.; besides alluding to other matters bearing upon the profession in which he was so deeply interested.

In the same letter, he writes that circumstances prevented his having his friend, Captain Bruce, for a companion, which was a great disappointment to him; but adds: "I had the pleasure of the company of Lieutenant Leahey, R.E.; and I believe it was ordered of God for our mutual good that we should travel together. I found him alive to, and anxious about, the concerns of his immortal soul: and after our day's work, we often read the Word of God and prayed together. This was a great pleasure to me, and, I trust, of benefit to us both.

"You will be glad to hear that, when I was at Florence, I made the acquaintance of the chief friend of the Madiai, who gave me a full account of those most interesting persons; and though he said he had but little hope of their being released prior to the expiration of their sentence, yet, he told me, they gloried in being counted worthy to suffer, not only shame, but cruel persecution, for the name of Jesus. He added that, notwithstanding the utmost efforts on the part of the Jesuits, backed by the government, neither in Florence nor in Rome itself were they able entirely to check the circulation of the Protestant Bible, or to eradicate the effects which, when read, it had produced on the minds and conduct of those who had received it. He also said that the spirit of religious inquiry was much on the increase in Italy. Is not this, my dear sir, glorious news? The hand of our God is not shortened, that it cannot save; neither is His ear heavy, that it cannot hear. May He accomplish His work in this benighted land, and thoroughly overcome the Man of sin, who, in this (so-called) Eternal City, in all his pride and pomp, 'setteth himself above all that is called God.' 'He is faithful that hath promised'—'who also will do it.' "

To the same friend, a few months later :—

"Portobello, Dublin, *April* 16, 1853.

"My dear Colonel,—Since your most kind letter of the 28th February arrived, I have been anxiously expecting the arrival of a schooner from Leghorn, on board of which I had placed one or two little packages for conveyance to England; and as there was, amongst other Italian curiosities, one which I purposed presenting to yourself, I deferred writing till I could make satisfactory mention concerning it. The vessel has just arrived in safety, and I therefore lose no time in forwarding to you what I hope you will kindly accept, as a very small token of the esteem and affection which I have long borne towards yourself and Mrs Anderson. It is a vase sculptured at Florence out of 'Verde Antica' marble; and it will afford me sincere pleasure should you deem it worthy of a place in that drawing-room where I have received so much kindness.

"Since I last wrote to you, Colonel Savage has been so kind as to appoint me his adjutant while he remains in command here, and I am now sanguine of being re-appointed when Colonel Warde arrives from Limerick, as my kind and much esteemed friend Colonel Armstrong has recommended me to him. It is an office of considerable responsibility, and at times the duties require much bodily and mental exertion, but I like it the better on these accounts, for one is always happier when one has plenty to employ one's mind; and

I humbly trust that God will give me grace and strength to fulfil these duties as becomes a good soldier, and a faithful servant of Christ. I was greatly obliged to you for taking so much trouble about my shot. I have determined to follow your advice, and have got twelve more shot and shells made. There are one or two alterations, and I hope improvements, in my plan. I am not a little sanguine of success. Before I went on leave to the Continent, I made trial of the principle with a rifle, and succeeded beyond my utmost expectations, so far as the experiments were carried on. I am about to resume them, and, on Thursday next, will practise at the Pigeon-house at long ranges, in order that I may be able to inform the select committee of the result of the trials of my invention, as far as I could carry them on with my own resources. Should the committee consent to the trial of my shot, I will avail myself of your very kind offer to watch for me the progress of these trials, as I think it is unlikely they will grant me leave during the summer for any purpose.

"During the past week, the usual April meetings of the Irish Clergy took place in the Rotunda. I had the privilege of attending three of the morning ones, when they all assembled for prayer and reading the Word of God at 7 A.M. We then breakfasted together, and re-assembled in the Rotunda to discuss various pre-arranged subjects. Several spoke admirably, but none more so than the Rev. E. Bickersteth. It was, indeed, delightful to hear those men of God telling of their experience during a long and laborious life in their Master's vineyard. We could not but feel our hearts warmed within us at the recital of so many interesting facts. I am convinced that these meetings are sources of great good to this land. I learned that those clergymen who attend them, some of whom were at first lukewarm, are every year becoming more interested in the great work now going on. Can you conceive a more encouraging sight than that of four hundred ministers of the Gospel coming together for the purpose of uniting in prayer to God, that He would carry on the work amongst us more effectually; whilst at the same time, an opportunity was afforded the aged and more experienced servants of Christ, to tell their younger brethren how they might best promote the interests of His kingdom. I must confess I never saw a more heart-stirring scene.

"I saw Fitzgerald the other day; he is now quite well, and his wife and infant are progressing favourably; he desired me to send his most affectionate regards. I have to thank you very much for your kind letter about the Horse-Artillery. I have not made, nor do I purpose making, any further application for an appointment than that which you recommended. If I get one, it will be altogether owing to your great kindness. Please give my kindest regards to Mrs Anderson and Harry, who, I suppose, is the only one of your family now with you. You must all miss your daughter much. Believe me, dear Colonel, your sincere young friend,   A. VANDELEUR."

During the two years that he was quartered in Ireland, Arthur Vandeleur had frequent opportunities of taking a personal interest in his tenantry. They were justly proud of his soldier-like spirit and high character. And whilst his kindly affections and generous sympathies drew out their warmest attachment, he became doubly sensible of his responsibilities as a landlord. Distinctly did he feel, that all that he had was his only to hold as a steward, for an unseen Master, to whom he must render a faithful account.

Besides his efforts to promote the comfort of the poor on the estate, by improving their cottages and gardens, and in other ways; he also established a school, and paid an able master for five years, in sanguine hope of a success which was never realised. During the whole of this time, the Romish priests would not allow their people to send a single child to the school, because the Bible was to be read there; although there was a distinct engagement that no controversial subject should be introduced.

This disappointment grieved him to the heart. But his personal influence, whenever he was able to be amongst his people, was irresistible. No priest could gainsay the truth and love of that honest, warm nature ; nor veil " the shining light " of that beautiful presence, and happy, holy life. The peasantry were deeply impressed by his earnest devotion to his Divine Master and Saviour, and would listen by the hour to the winning tones of his pleasant voice, as he sought with all the fervour and fire of his heart, to persuade them to come to Jesus for pardon and peace. Many of them still speak of him with tears, and exclaim, " Ah, he was too good to live ! The Lord loved him too much to spare him to us any longer."

"The memory of the just is blessed."

CHAPTER VIII.

The Camp.

"His love possessing, I am blest;
    Secure, whatever change may come:
Whether I go to east or west,
    With Him I shall be still at home."

DEEP in every English heart lies the memory of the Crimean war. The first storm oversweeping a sky of forty years' serenity, startled a tranquil country into an enthusiasm of military ardour, and of chivalrous sympathy with her noble and gallant soldiers.

None can forget the tremendous excitement and emotion stirred by the first tidings of the battle of the Alma; how a conquering nation walked in pride, whilst loving hearts were trembling in dread suspense until the list of the names of the wounded and the slain crushed them with anguish; or, by its blessed omissions, filled them with joyful thanksgiving.

It was then that Arthur Vandeleur, and hundreds of other young Englishmen who had grown up in the long summer of peace, knowing war but in name, found themselves for the first time face to face with a hostile army. And it fell to Arthur's hand to fire the first shot at the foe. He rode beside the foremost gun up the slope at the affair of Bulgarnac, the day before the battle of the Alma. It was his first step in a career of gallantry—a career shared by such numbers as hardly to be remarkable. Yet, in allusion to his conduct throughout that campaign, General Anderson writes: "Vandeleur was a living proof that there is nothing incompatible in being a noble and chivalrous soldier, and a warm and earnest Christian. He served in the Crimea under that distinguished officer Captain (now Colonel) Maude; and quite bore out the expectations I had formed of his proving an ornament to his profession. He was in all the actions in which Captain Maude's troop was engaged; and I received a letter from a lieutenant-colonel in the Artillery, whilst in the Crimea, in which were these memorable words: 'Vandeleur, I love. He is brave as a lion; a polished gentleman, and, above all, a devoted Christian.'"

The troop of Horse-Artillery to which he belonged, under the command of Captain Maude, had embarked in the *Sultana*, at Woolwich Dockyard, on the 25th of April 1854, and entered the Dardanelles on the 4th of June.

The residence of our troops at Varna, the landing on the Russian shore, with the whole of the Crimean campaign, are now only chapters in an old and oft-repeated story. Very slight extracts will therefore suffice, from Mr Vandeleur's correspondence upon subjects of military interest; and from his diary, which is a complete history of the war, given with considerable force, and great distinctness of detail.

TO CAPTAIN BRUCE.

"Camp Devna, Bulgaria,
July 17, 1854.

". . . . You may easily imagine to how great an
extent this kind of life militates against our growth in
grace; we are thrown together so constantly, and have
so many little trifles to annoy us, that our tempers are
much tried. I find the use and the comfort now more
than ever, of the 'Thoughts of Peace,' and Bogatzky's
'Golden Treasury,' and Newton's 'Cardiphonia.' The
great pleasure I derive from the perusal of the first of
these, I have to thank you for, and the dear Colonel,
for the benefit and help of the last two. I hope you
continue to read the 'Thoughts' as we arranged.
That for to-day is very beautiful, No. 157, page 207:
'Thus saith the Lord, like as I have brought all this
great trial upon this people, so will I bring upon them
all the good that I have promised them.' Well may
we say, 'Faithful is He that hath promised, who also will
do it.' I much feel the want of Christian intercourse, to
keep eternal things more before my eyes. The things of
this world at times seem to shut them almost out of
my sight. Once I thought myself grateful to my Lord
for His great mercy to me, but I fear He has found
my gratitude only as the morning dew—soon passed
away; still my trust is in His word, 'I will never leave

thee, nor forsake thee.' Hammond of the Rifle Brigade is almost the only person I have met, with whom I could converse freely. I had a long ride with him a few days since, and enjoyed it excessively. The weather cool, the scenery exquisite, and a real Christian for my companion, could it be otherwise than delightful?

"Would that you were here. Absence teaches me the value of a true friend. I often think, were you here, I should prize you more and trust you better than I have ever done before. Now for some account of myself and my doings. We have been here nearly three weeks—at Devna, nineteen miles north of Varna. This place is well suited for an encampment, being a large plain seven miles by two, surrounded by low mountains, covered with brushwood, and with a small river running through the centre. The whole of the cavalry and ourselves occupy the north of the river, the Light Brigade and the rest of the Artillery, the high ground on the other side. It is said that this plain is hotter in summer and colder in winter than any other part of Turkey: and I quite believe it, for I can answer for a tolerable degree of *heat*, having seen the thermometer in my tent one day at 102°; however, this intense heat does not last long, but we find the sudden and great changes very trying, a variation of 40° between mid-day and midnight being not uncommon. . . . . . We have at present nothing to do but drill, and provide food for ourselves and our horses. You may laugh, but neither of these is such an easy operation as you suppose, as you would soon find out were you a subaltern on duty. Watering-order three times a-day, and two hours grazing at some distance from the camp twice a-day; barley to be cut in its green state and carried home; with stable-duty as at Woolwich, and the poor subaltern when on duty has but little time to do anything but eat his meals; however, on other days, when drill and camp-mess are over, there is little to be done, so we ride into the country on exploring expeditions, and sketch, or hunt the wild dogs across the plain; the latter is getting a very favourite amusement, and one generally finds fifteen or twenty horsemen, in very motley costumes, drawn out to the meet. The dogs are forbidden to be killed, being the scavengers of the district, and therefore these gallops generally end harmlessly. . . . . . We all have little ponies about thirteen hands, of all shapes and colours. I have been extremely fortunate, (?) and bought for £10 (£5 being the average price here,) an Arab, universally allowed to be the handsomest in the army,—he certainly is a perfect beauty. Should he and I live, I hope to bring 'Omer Pasha' to England. . . . . . I expect soon to be promoted, I trust not, however, till we have met the enemy. I shall try and get some months' leave, if promoted, and get home, if there is nothing doing here. Suppose you try to get leave at the same time, and join me somewhere in these countries—how I should rejoice. Adieu my beloved friend. God bless you and keep you ! Ever yours,

" A. VANDELEUR."

" CAMP DEVNA, August 27, 1854.

" MY DEAR MR FLEURY,—I am indeed obliged for your most kind and welcome letter, which arrived by last mail ; you can hardly imagine how much a friendly letter enlivens and cheers one's drooping spirits in these desolate, inhospitable regions. . . . . This is, indeed, a dry and barren land, where no water is, both physically and spiritually ; and when we see in the distance the peculiar balance-draw-wells of the country, which can be discerned a long way off, the chances are, that we find, to our disappointment, either the wells empty or the buckets broken off, which makes one feel the force of the simile employed by St Peter to describe the false prophets of his day—' Wells without water.' True emblems also of the ' prophets ' of this country. You, I am sure, must know well the lamentable state of infidelity and ignorance in which these people live. They ignorantly worship an unknown God, and deny altogether the only revelation He has ever given of Himself. . . . . There is, I understand, not a single Christian missionary in the country, with the exception of one or two sent to the Greeks and the Armenians.

" It is the greatest pity to see a magnificent country,

such as this naturally is, running to waste in every direction. God has given it natural capabilities far above those of most countries, perhaps of any, and, as is too often the case, man works in exactly the inverse ratio. . . . . I have seen acres and acres of thistles seven and eight feet high, and so close that you can hardly walk between them. Every hedge is composed of the bushes which are so abundant everywhere— all thorns—and the most common weed by the way-side is a little thorn bush, somewhat resembling young gooseberry bushes. The cultivation, such as it is, is of the rudest description ; and I imagine the quantity of land under cultivation does not exceed one-fifth of the whole surface. This, then, being the country in which I have been living for nearly three months, will account, in some degree, for my not having written to you long since, because I really had nothing interesting to tell you, and will shew how acceptable letters from one's friends must be, as breaking, in a delightful manner, our dull routine of campaigning life.

"An attack of the combined fleets and armies on Sebastopol has at last been evidently determined on, and we are on our march from Jani-Vaza in Shumla, where we have been for the last month, to Varna, there to embark and take our share in the expedition. I trust and pray that the Lord of hosts may be on our side ; if so, 'through Him shall we do valiantly, for He it is that shall tread down all our enemies.' I am confident in the result being such as we could wish for, because I know that thousands of earnest Christians are striving with the Lord in prayer for us.

"One thing is necessary above all others to me, and to all here at the present moment—to prepare to meet our God. Oh, may He to whom alone the future is fully revealed, lead me and all of us to put all our trust in the merits and blood of His beloved Son; then, indeed, may we look forward with perfect confidence, and do our duty, even in the battle-field, as unto the Lord and not unto men, heartily and cheerfully. But, oh! what difficulties do we encounter in living to God anywhere. At home, there are the charms of the world and the host of Satan's allurements to pleasure, ease, and vanity; here, where removed in some degree from contact with these things, he takes another line, and tempts us to become selfish, overbearing, disagreeable, and unhappy, discontented with ourselves and with everything around us, ... as if we came out here to enjoy ourselves, and for that alone. We have, to be sure, suffered a good many privations, and our work has been very severe. For instance, I have never tasted good bread since I have been in the country, and we have often been many hours without food; our breakfasts have often consisted of tea without milk, some black bread, and raw onions; and our dinner, sometimes, of tough beef and biscuit. This is all owing to the difficulty of procuring transport. . . . . We marched from Devna yesterday with the 11th Hussars, and we are now encamped within two miles of Varna, overlooking the bay, which is very full of shipping. At last we know that we are destined for Sebastopol. * * * * With kind regards to Mrs Fleury and all your family, believe me to remain, with great regard, very sincerely yours,

" ARTHUR VANDELEUR."

CHAPTER IX.

Active Service.

"We climb'd the hard-won heights at length,
  Baptized in flame and fire,
And saw the foeman's sullen strength
  Which grimly made retire.

"Saw close at hand—then saw more far
  Amidst the batt'ry's smoke,
The ridges of his scatter'd war
  That broke, and ever broke."

"*Thursday, August 31st.*—Late last evening Maude returned with orders for us to embark in the *Pyrenees*, No. 1; *Kenilworth*, No. 40; *Harbinger*, No. 61; and *Burmah*, No. 85. This news caused universal joy, and will do wonders towards our recovery. I already feel better; the strong coffee *à la mode Turque* doing wonders for me. Shakespear was taken ill last night with fever, and has gone into Varna to Mr Angel's, of the post-office.

"*Friday, September 1st.*—Embarked yesterday, with two guns, two waggons, and fifty-four horses, in the *Pyrenees*.

"*Saturday, September 2nd.*—Like the ship very well, also the captain and chief officers. Plenty of room for men and horses—accommodation not as good as that of the *Sultana*—only two spare stalls. We are the only troop who have brought their baggage animals; all owing to Maude's good management."

"*Wednesday, 6th.*—This morning took a sketch of the fleets at anchor. On the look-out the whole day for the signal to weigh anchor, but none made."

In the evening, signal made from the *Emperor* for all agents, and shortly afterwards another, 'Prepare for sea to-morrow morning.' This set our minds at rest for the night. Yesterday I paid a visit to De Havilland, and was delighted to have once more the opportunity of reading and praying with him. How thankful I ought to be!

"*Thursday, 7th.*—About half-past seven the move became general. The French and Turkish fleets also got under way, and being to the east of us, were ahead for some time. Their steamers had three, four, and five vessels astern, and were much more scattered than our fleet. At one, we passed astern of them, apparently to let them get on our right;—wind favourable for Sebastopol—a gentle breeze and beautiful day—an auspicious beginning—may the end exceed our most sanguine expectations! A more magnificent sight it is impossible to conceive—we are all keeping our places beautifully, moving along about six miles an hour, convoyed by our three-deckers and the rest of our magnificent fleet. What an assemblage of power!—the two finest fleets in the world—numerous representatives of our splendid merchant navy, led by the best of our merchant steamers—these having on board 60,000 men, all in excellent health and high spirits. Well may the Russians take shelter in their strong forts, under cover of their numerous artillery.

"*Friday, Sept. 8th.*—Found ourselves at daylight

several miles short of our rendezvous;—many ships were out of sight—went very slowly to let them come up. At 11 A.M., came up with the French and Turkish fleets,—had to close-in to keep clear of them. They were all lying to on the port tack; they amounted to about twenty sail of the line, and a dozen frigates. We passed very close to them, and could see their decks crowded with soldiers. It was a glorious sight—out of sight of land, the sea perfectly smooth, and sur-rounded by ships and steamers of all kinds and sizes.

" Our rendezvous disappointed us sadly; we expected to have seen No. 9 (13 miles west of Sebastopol) made, and we are losing all patience at our slow rate of pro-gression. The band of the 95th, on board, is a great acquisition, and enlivens us every evening,—Irish and French airs predominating. My horses are doing famously, and the men are quiet and attentive,—the sick improving. Have been reading the Life of Dr Gordon attentively, and admire it excessively; it affords a convincing proof that all great minds do not reject religion. He studied the theory and evidence of Christianity very deeply, became convinced of their truth; and also saw that head knowledge availed little. In this state he remained a long time, but at length was enabled to go as a little child to Jesus, to cast all his care upon Him,—and felt joy and peace in believing. From that time forth, his life, always useful in no ordinary degree, was devoted to his God, and the conversations which took place during his last long illness, are edifying, and deeply interesting. Oh, that I were more like him, unselfish, active, and benevolent!

"Jesus, beloved Saviour! grant that I may become so, more and more every day I live."

"*Sept.* 12*th.*—Sighted the Crimea at daybreak,—kept steady course until 4 P.M.,—then altered course to N. by W., and continued so for one hour, when the *Emperor* again steered E., and we all followed her;—land right a-head, at $5\frac{1}{4}$,—stood in for it,—men-of-war getting to the front,—*Arethusa* leading in a dashing manner. Most of them anchored about eight miles off shore; we held on and anchored, in the order specified, at 7 P.M. A most beautiful sunset, the last rays of the sun shooting through innumerable summer clouds of singular loveliness,—a fine sandy beach, and grass land behind. A town in sight, and forts at the water's edge (uncertain)."

"*Thursday, Sept.* 14*th.*—Started at four o'clock this morning, and moved again twenty miles down the coast, nearer to Sebastopol; anchored at nine, having got into a nice mess just before,—the *Simla, Pyrenees, Colombo,* and *London* all together running foul of each other. Fortunately the sea was smooth as glass, and hardly a breath of wind stirring, so they got clear without damage. The French landed first, and immediately planted the *Tricolor*. About two miles to our right, our first boat reached the land twenty minutes after, right opposite us,—7th Fusiliers and some Sappers in her. Many more followed immediately. No Russian troops in sight, except a Cossack officer, and three of his men, quietly surveying us from the shore with a telescope. Herds of cattle, and plenty of hay to be seen, and a village about five miles off,—a lake immediately behind the landing place. We are about seventeen miles from Sebastopol.

"*Friday, Sept. 15th.*—The men on shore suffered a good deal from the weather during the night, as they had no tents. A heavy surf rolled on shore, and the ships rode so uneasily that it was deemed inexpedient to land the horses, and accordingly the signal was made for some of the cavalry and artillery transports to prepare to get under way; towards mid-day, however, the surf abated so much that it was determined to land us, and we commenced disembarking at half-past one o'clock, having previously put all our carriages into a boat or flat, and taken them out again. When we got to the beach with my No. 2 gun and fourteen horses, the surf was still high, but the horses stood it famously, though we were detained in it for upwards of half-an-hour, by the stage on which they were to run out of the boats unshipping. At last we secured it, and the sailors, tar-like, stripped, and taking the breakers one by one, swam ashore to draw up the flat.   No accident of any kind occurred; the sailors took the horses and ran them down, our men pushing them from behind.   At half-past three, I first set foot on the enemy's land.   May the good and gracious Lord bless, preserve, and keep me while here! In thousands of ways He has blessed me.   Oh that I may seek to glorify His name, may watch and pray that I enter not into temptation!   We landed No. 1 gun just before dark, and had hard work, getting all square for the night; but the men worked famously, and by ten I got to my tent, which we had taken care to bring on shore, and three more for the men.   The night was fine, and we were undisturbed.

"*Saturday, September* 16*th.*—All astir early—made inquiries after water, which, it appears, is *very* scarce— nobody knew anything about it; so I went with my men, in fatigue dress, saddles, and swords, in search of some.   Saw Colonel Strangways.   Went up the hill to the right, and out towards the Light Division.   Saw the French and our men getting water at the upper end of the lake, and went there.   Waded through much mud, and when we tried to water our horses, sank in the mud; so I turned about and went to a village two miles further off, and there got water.   Fed with corn in the fields.   When returning, the Duke of Cambridge spoke to me about the horses, and admired their condition. When I got back, after a twelve-mile ride, found we were wanted to go out with Lord Cardigan and all the cavalry, to make a forced reconnaissance. Got ready in marching order—three days' provisions—and started at 1 P.M. His Lordship took us fourteen miles in an east by north direction, over a country as flat as a billiard-table, without a ravine or hillock of any kind, or any water;—crossed an arm of the sea. Cavalry leading, guns ready to open while they crossed—a village within range, where Cossacks were supposed to be. Entered the village; only one or two Turks to be seen. Went on to another village, the plain gently rising, till we attained the top, and had a most extensive view. I never saw so uninteresting a country. We could see as far as the Putrid Sea, with a horizon as level as the sea itself, and twenty or thirty miles towards the south-east. Not a Cossack to be seen. A Turk said that three days before, twelve thousand Russian cavalry had passed through towards Sebastopol. (Don't believe a word of it, as they could get no water in such a country.) An officer set the example of plundering ducks and geese, which our men were not slow to follow. I forbade it, and made them disgorge. We afterwards bought a few very cheap—one turkey, four ducks, and one chicken, for two shillings. Eggs fourteen a-penny. I thought this good, but we have been outdone. Lieutenant Taddy having purchased fourteen pigs for a piastre (twopence)!!! Remained an hour at this village, and returned by the same road, which appeared endless, now the chance of fighting was gone.

"*Sunday, September 17th.*—What a Sabbath-day was this! Work, work all day. No time for anything but work. Thank God, He enabled me sometimes to think of His goodness, and to bless His name! Saw Captain Anderson in the evening, and was delighted to have a few words of serious and profitable conversation with him; he told me he now longed more than ever to glorify God, and to live for Him. May his prayers be answered, for Jesus' sake!

"*Monday, September 18th.*—Busy getting all in order for to-morrow's march. Six horses joined to fill up vacancies.

"*Tuesday, September 19th.*—Marched at 6 A.M., and formed in order of march at the outposts, with the rest of the army. Cavalry leading, I Troop supporting them,—the several divisions of infantry in double column of divisions, according to seniority, — rifles bringing up the rear. Four miles before us we saw our enemies, the Russians. At first a few Cossacks, but presently heavy columns of cavalry, were seen just behind the hills. We crossed a little rivulet—guns by a bridge—cavalry and infantry fording. The cavalry were then ordered up the hill, and disappeared from our sight. Presently our troop and Captain Brandling's (C) were ordered up to support Lord Lucan and his two squadrons, which consisted of 8th, 11th, and

13th. When we got to the top, we found on the opposite ridge several masses of cavalry, with skirmishers out, prepared to dispute our further progress;—they were about two thousand two hundred yards off. We formed line to the front, and halted for a few minutes, while the cavalry advanced eight hundred yards, to allow time for the infantry to come up;—we had some rifles with us. The infantry came up quickly, and formed line two hundred yards behind us;—while this was going on the cavalry advanced still further, throwing out skirmishers; and the affair commenced by the enemy's skirmishers, twice as numerous, firing at them. They did not reply, being out of range of carbines. Our two squadrons formed across the road; presently down came ten guns and began firing at our squadrons at nine hundred yards' range. Lord Raglan refused to allow the Horse-Artillery to fire, as he said it would bring on a general action; however, after several casualties among the cavalry, he consented. We galloped to the front, with C Troop, and came into action—range rather long—however we peppered them well; our first shot, fired by No. 2, pitched into a gun, and caused a quick retreat from it—so the staff say. We then limbered up, and moved to the left, having silenced the guns after a round or two, and caused them to retreat with the cavalry. The enemy extended their right, in order to outflank us, but were now without guns; so we pitched shot and shell right into their masses, and again caused them to retreat out of range to the next ridge. Their guns were 8 or 12-pounders, and the shot came bounding along through our sub-divisions, and over our heads; however, (thank God!) *we* suffered no loss. Five amputations were performed upon poor fellows of the cavalry, and they lost five horses. One shell burst in the stomach of a horse—we found on the field four men and five horses dead of the enemy, but afterwards ascertained that their casualties amounted to thirty-two men and thirty-five horses. This action goes by the name of 'the Cavalry Affair of Bulgarnac.'

" *Wednesday, September 20th.*—We marched from our encampment at Bulgarnac at 9 A.M.—passed several dead men and horses where the Russian guns had been. At eleven we arrived within three miles of the Russian army, and halted for half-an-hour, while our generals reconnoitred their position. It was evidently one of enormous strength, and was well chosen, as the Russians had every advantage over their opponents. The river Alma flowed along their entire front; and on its banks were the upper, lower, and middle villages of Alma. Trees and vineyards abound-ed also, and tended to conceal the enemy's riflemen, while they seriously impeded our advance. On the other side of the river the ground sloped upwards in a kind of natural glacis for three quarters of a mile. The heights were crowned with intrenchments, and defended by many guns. On the left of their position the ground was very precipitous, and on their right it sloped gently off; but the river was deeper higher up, and we could not turn their right without becoming separated from the French. It was, with great judgment, determined to attack in front; for the French, who were on the right, had thus the support of their steamers, which shelled the heights opposite their right flank most beautifully during the whole of the attack, at a range of about 3000 yards. The Turks, 7000 strong, supported, or formed the French reserve. We had the post of honour given to us, on the left of our allies, to attack the village of Alma, and storm the strongest part of the Russian position, where all their intrenchments were, and the greater part of their forces drawn up. The strength of the Russian army is estimated at 40,000 infantry, 12,000 cavalry, and 108 guns. The battle began by the advance of the French at half-past twelve o'clock, the fleet shelling the Russian heights. We were halted just out of range, and had time to admire the glorious scene. The sun shone with unclouded rays; which, (reflected from thousands of bayonets, swords, helmets, and ornaments,) together with the celerity of the French movements, the steadiness of the Russians, and the imposing, yet quiet, appearance of our own columns, presented a scene seldom to be equalled, never excelled. The French shells burst with wondrous accuracy, which called forth continuous expressions of astonishment : they must have done great execution. The English ships looked on in dignified silence. At last, when the French had had half-an-hour's start of us, the order to stand to our arms was passed along our columns, and we were instantly in the saddle. We had not advanced many hundred yards, when a 24-pounder shot came booming along, and the white wreath of smoke ascended from the centre intrenchment, which commanded several roads. It only just reached us, and did no harm. Presently Minié bullets began to whiz about us rather thick, and the order was given for the columns of attack to deploy into line ; the Rifles, as skirmishers, getting well to the front. The enemy's Riflemen were covered by the trees, and walls of the villages ; but though ours were at first entirely without cover, they quickly forced the former to retreat across the river. The Light and 1st Divisions formed the first line—the 7th Fusiliers on the right, and the Highlanders on the left. The 2nd and 3rd Divisions formed the second line, and the 4th in reserve. The Field Batteries and C Troop were with their respective Divisions ; the Cavalry in two lines on the left, with our troop of Royal Horse-Artillery.

"The enemy's guns were of very large calibre, and were well served, the ranges well known, and the ground marked with posts. Their shot reached to great distances, and did much execution. We lost a shaft horse from a 12-pound shot when we were on the extreme left—the range must have been, at least, three thousand yards. Our Riflemen having splendidly driven back the Russian skirmishers to the other side of the river, the line advanced to its edge, and our field batteries, which had till then been silent, opened a heavy and effective fire, under cover of which our men crossed the river with a rush, and re-formed under the steep bank at the other side, where they were, to some extent, defended from the severe artillery fire from the intrenchments. Between the bank and these intrenchments was a sloping plateau of, at least, twelve hundred yards, but nothing daunted, our incomparable infantry, having re-formed, and had a moment's breathing time, suddenly appeared in line on its further edge, and, led in the most gallant style by their officers, the 19th, 23rd, 33rd and 95th rushed up the slope.

"Instantly grape and cannister poured through and through them, sweeping down whole sections at a time. They broke, but not to turn ; on, onwards they pressed, halting only occasionally for an instant to make some return in answer to the dreadful fire which had now decimated their ranks. At this critical moment, when our fire from the north side of the river was necessarily becoming more slack for fear of injuring our own men, a battery (Captain Turner's) having succeeded in crossing to the other side, galloped up the slope on their flank, and began to enfilade, with a most effective

fire, the guns in the main intrenchment. The fire of
the latter now gradually slackened, and the Russians
began to remove their guns and retire. Some, however,
still remained, and our gallant red-coats, feeling the
good effects of Captain Turner's movements, again
rushed on, stormed the intrenchment, put every Russian
to the sword, and took two guns. Great was the cheering from the whole army when the British colours
floated from the parapet of the work. At this time
the French appeared on the top of the hill to the right,
and began to fire on the Russian columns in retreat,
but from some unexplained cause they left off firing in
a very short time, and thus only rendered half the
assistance they might have done. While all this battle
was going on, we were kept standing at ease on the
left flank, watching a very large body of the enemy's
cavalry on the other side of the river; now, however, the order at last arrived for us to advance, and
down we went at a trot, through the upper village of
Alma, and along a narrow lane, the intrenchment at the
top of the hill right opposite still firing shot and shell.
In this lane, unfortunately to all appearance, but not
so as it afterwards turned out, two of our guns upset,
and delayed us for ten minutes. No. 1 gun which got
through safe was thus detained on our side of the river
and under cover of the steep bank of the other side.
While there, we saw several shells burst in the very
ravine we were to have gone through ;—this firing lasted

the whole time we were waiting for the gun, and ceased just as we got the order to advance. Up we went with the 11th, and, when on the plateau, pushed our horses into a gallop, and away we went at a rattling pace. We got to the top just in time, and saw a column of infantry and artillery retiring up the ravine in front about eleven hundred yards off. We came into action at once, and plied them with shot and shell for a quarter of an hour and did great execution. We were the only artillery that fired on this column, and yet the next day we found there upwards of two hundred dead bodies; so that allowing for the proportion of wounded, their loss at this point must have been great. That they suffered severely from our fire was evident, because, though in retreat, they brought a 12-pounder battery into action on the opposite ridge, out of range of our 6-pounders, and began to fire at us; not, however, before we had ceased firing at their column as being out of range, and were limbering up to retire.

"Captain Maude begged of Lord Lucan and Sir Colin Campbell to be allowed to advance down the hill, but Sir Colin said Lord Raglan's positive orders were that no one should go beyond the ridge on which we then were. Had we then been allowed to advance with the cavalry, we must have taken many guns and prisoners, and inflicted severe loss on their rear. Neither Wellington nor Napoleon would have stopped short at this point.

" When we retired, we found the Highlanders in line on our flank, they cheered us lustily, to which we as heartily responded. The Duke of Cambridge, who witnessed our advance up the slope, told General Strangways that Captain Maude's troop came up the hill and into action in the most gallant style. After resting for half-an-hour, and feeding, we again advanced,—the Russians being sufficiently far off,—went down the hill, and up the next ridge more to the right ; the whole army soon followed, and we found ourselves on a table-land seven miles by one-and-a-half. The Russians had now re-formed on the nearest line of hills ; no pursuit was allowed, and we retired to rest, tired out with our day's work, and deeply thankful to Him who had given to our arms so glorious a victory."

" *Thursday, September* 21*st.*—Having hurt my leg a good deal, and suffered much pain, was scarcely able to go from our camp at all to-day. The field of battle was still strewed with dead, wounded, and dying men. Many of the 33rd regiment were without medical assistance during the whole night. As for the poor Russians who thickly covered the ground at all the principal points, they, of course, had to wait till our own men had been attended to, and most patiently they endured their dreadful sufferings. One group I went to with our surgeon, consisted of five, out of which number four had to undergo amputations ; yet they sat or lay together, without uttering a groan, or shewing the least impatience. I assisted Thornton to take off a leg, holding the arteries, while he tied them.

"Despatches with the news of the victory were this day sent home, but we were unable to write, having so much to do. The bodies of English and Russians—foes while living—now lay peacefully together in every conceivable attitude of death. In the main intrenchment at least five hundred were lying together. Some had both hands clasped in the attitude of prayer, one with his left arm broken, had the right extended upwards as if he prayed. . . . . . It was a sickening and horrible sight ; and I rode away, now fully impressed with a sense of the awful calamity of war. May God in His goodness teach us to be merciful to our enemies, and soon bring to a close this awful war."

"*Monday, September 25th.*—Marched at 8 A.M. along the main road, turned to the left about three miles from the fortress, and went along a very narrow road, making it wider with our wheels. The road led through the bush. The cavalry soon took the wrong road, which Maude found out at once, and halted his troop. Providential it was that he did so, for had he gone on without escort, we should have found ourselves, with six guns, opposed to the rear-guard of Menschikoff's army. He sent me back to inform Lord Raglan, but I missed him in the wood, and galloped back along the road, looking for him. I retraced my steps to a house where I had last seen him, and there asked which road Lord Raglan had taken. They all said he went down the road to the left, which I thought very odd; but, with an officer on the Quartermaster-General's Staff, I went down. He presently stopped to water his horse; I rode on, and at last found myself *in* Sebastopol, at the head of the harbour, not five hundred yards from one of their steamers. I was quite astonished, and looked around me in wonder. There was a long low line of fortification before me, about a thousand yards off. As I stopped my horse to look, three Minié bullets came whistling about me, and I heard the reports not far off. I put spurs to my horse, and galloped off round the corner. When I got back to the troop, I found them about one mile in advance of where I had left them, and was told that the Russians were in force in our front, and not more than three hundred yards off. The guns were at once brought into action, but we found that the enemy was retreating.

"*Tuesday, September 26th.*—Marched to Balaklava, and encamped amongst vineyards and orchards. Balaklava taken chiefly by C. Troop.

"*Wednesday, September 27th.*—Marched up to the heights of Sebastopol. The whole army made a demonstration above the town. Got into a comfortable residence and outhouses. It had been sacked by the Cossacks, and all the furniture destroyed.

"*Thursday, September 28th.*—Russians fire occasionally at our lines.

"*Friday, September 29th.*—Went up the hill with General Burgoyne, to make a reconnaissance, within two thousand yards of the fortress. As we were advancing, General Airey was sent for by Lord Raglan, and the reconnaissance was at an end. Russians threatening our rear."

"*Sunday, October 1st.*—Maude read service at our bivouac at the Poplars."

"*Tuesday, October 3rd.*—Ordered back to Balaklava, Lord Raglan wanting our house for headquarters. Our troop required to protect the cavalry."

"*Saturday, October 7th.*—An orderly galloped round by our camp at $5\frac{1}{2}$ A.M., ordering us to turn out at once, our outposts being engaged. We were on parade in twenty minutes. Advanced with all the cavalry to the front, our videttes firing all the time. Our outposts at last retired. We were halted for a quarter of an hour under cover of the ridge, while Lord Lucan and staff went forward to reconnoitre. We were presently ordered up by Maude. The moment the Russians saw our now well-known troop coming over the hill, they turned and *fled*;—twelve hundred cavalry retreating before six guns. We came quickly into action, and gave them a round or two, but the distance was too great. We then directed our attention to five hundred more on the hill opposite, and fired; but some of the staff calling out, ' These are French,' we left off firing, and they retreated in time. The cavalry are much disgusted with this affair. Lord Lucan has ordered a parade for the cavalry and our troop every morning at 5 A.M."

CHAPTER X.

The Hospital.

<blockquote>

"Hast Thou not given Thy word
  To save my soul from death !
And I can trust my Lord
  To keep my mortal breath.
    I'll go and come,
    Nor fear to die,
    Till from on high
    Thou call me home."

</blockquote>

ON the 19th of October, Mr Vandeleur was seized with a scrious attack of fever and ague; and on the 21st, was sent on board the *Shooting Star*, off Bala-klava.

"*Tuesday, October 24th.*—Spent a most awful night, —frightful dreams. When I awoke, felt quite paralyzed; unable to move hand or foot; began to be alarmed about myself, but found great comfort when I thought of the promises of God to me, and His great mercy hitherto. This made me trust Him now with all my heart.

"*Wednesday, October 25th*—A sad day for the army. Troops on parade as usual at five. The parade was about to break up at eight, when the videttes began to circle right and left, and immediately retired. The Russians were now seen coming in force on our right front, and the Turks (the cowardly rascals) in charge of the five forts on the ridge and hills, left all our guns loaded, and bolted without even firing a shot, or spiking a single gun. The Russians of course at once took possession of all these forts, and turned the magnificent guns in them upon us, and pounded us well. This was a severe and dreadful blow to us, who depended on the Turks keeping them against any odds. How misplaced was our confidence, the result proved; and dearly bought was the experience. The Russian cavalry, encouraged by this unexpected success, now advanced boldly in great force, at least five or six thousand strong, and were supported by the fire of the forts. The only artillery we had at first, to oppose them, was our troop and Barker's Battery; we opened fire at once upon them, and of course with effect; our cavalry now formed up in line, charged them successively by regiments, and at last succeeded in driving them back. Nothing could exceed the gallantry of our cavalry, or the impetuosity of their charges, they fought the foe for the first time to-day. The Greys were particularly remarked during two splendid charges. Having driven the cavalry back with loss, we now began to feel the effects of the fire of the redoubts, and the cavalry were ordered to retake them. A strange order! Cavalry to retake forts!! However, our Light Brigade went at them, and succeeded in getting three of them from the enemy, but the guns were gone, our splendid guns! thirty guns taken of ours! Enough to break an artilleryman's heart, and all through those rascals, the Turks.

"*Thursday, October 26th.*—Sailed from Balaklava for Scutari."

Mr Vandeleur arrived at Scutari Hospital, seriously ill; and was entirely disabled from returning to active service until the following December.

As strength began to return, he resumed his journal, and united his testimony with thousands of others, to the wonder-working genius and self-sacrificing benevolence of that noble and heroic woman, whose name is ever breathed by the British soldier with blessings which find an echo in every British heart.

Who can read the oft-told story, and not pray, God bless FLORENCE NIGHTINGALE! God grant her, if yet it may be, renewed health for a continuance of her devoted labours for the soldier's benefit. Or, if that be denied to a nation's prayers, God grant to her, who, "in feeding the lamp of charity," has well-nigh exhausted the lamp of life, in the darkness of her chamber of sickness, to realise the glorious presence of her Divine Redeemer; the Man who has suffered, the God who saves.

"*Saturday, December 2nd.*—Still at Scutari, and in the same room with Maude and Yates—Yates very ill with low fever. Anxious to get back to the Crimea, as I now feel quite well. Applied for a passage to Major Sillery, and sent in a medical certificate of my recovery from Mr Munn, who has been so very kind and attentive to us all. No vessel going up.

"*Sunday, December 3rd.*—Enjoyed the inestimable

privilege of again partaking of the Holy Communion—service read by Mr Sabin, Mr Freeman, and Mr Lawless. Two of the clergymen now attached to the hospital are, I know, excellent men, who devote themselves to the welfare and comfort of the sufferers. There are seven chaplains here, and eleven with the army."

" *Wednesday, December 6th.*—Went to see Taswell in the hospital—great difficulty in finding him ;—he is fast recovering, and very cheerful. While there, Miss Nightingale appeared outside, attended by one of her nurses, and talked for some time to a wounded man of the 13th Light Dragoons. No one in the room but myself had seen her. She is no enthusiast, but a woman of uncommon energy of mind, and strength of character; no one can help admiring and respecting her, for she devotes her whole time and attention to the work of charity which she has undertaken; and a wonderful reformation has taken place in almost every department since her arrival. She has shirts distributed to all new comers,—clean sheets given to those who require them—has engaged cooks for the sick officers, so that they can have everything they wish for, cooked at any hour; and many similar improvements have taken place.

" *Thursday, December 7th.*—Mrs Morris, wife of Captain Morris, 17th Lancers, so very kind to me to-day. Though a perfect stranger, she gave me two tins of chocolate and a basin, and some silks, &c., to take to the Crimea, saying she had brought them for her husband, but being of no use to him, as he returns home, I might have them. Captain Hastings of the *Curaçoa*, also most kindly offered me a passage with him to the Crimea, and told me to be on board on Saturday morning. This I most gladly accepted.

"*Friday, December 8th.*—Busy shopping, and preparing for my departure to-morrow. Tins of marmalade, pots of anchovy, and other pastes, tongues, biscuits, sauces, butter, and chocolate, being the edibles; fur coats, India-rubber coat, long boots of Russian leather, being the clothing most in request. Got also a cotton-wool quilt, a substitute for eider down; bought also a pair of long boots for Anderson—capital things. Cavalry soldiers ought to have no others. It would be much better, too, if the infantry soldier had something of the same kind, only made of lighter material, and not to come up so high. At camp the mud is almost knee-deep, and they find it next to impossible to dry their trousers.

"*Saturday, December 9th.*—Packed up my traps, and went on board H.M. Steam Frigate *Curaçoa*, 31 guns, at 9 A.M.—we sailed at twelve. Captain Hastings exceedingly kind, has given me half of his outer cabin to myself, and makes me dine with him. I swing my cot in the evening at eight, and it is taken down before breakfast.

"*Sunday, December 10th.*—Towed a ship through

thé Bosphorus.   Making 9·8 knots this morning, having set fore and aft sails.   At noon, one hundred miles from Balaklava.   The captain has prayers every morning and evening.

"To-day we had service at 10½ A.M.   He makes attendance voluntary.   Few sailors came, but all the officers, boys, and most of the marines, were present. Service full, except Litany—impressively read by the chaplain, and short sermon.   It is a delightful thing to see those in such absolute authority aiming in all they do to glorify God.   Captain Hastings is indeed a Christian man : kind and affable in his manner—no quarter-deck humbug—and much unaffected humility. Sunday School for the Naval Cadets in the chaplain's cabin—what an example !   He lent me a valuable work on Christian retirement ; by whom, I know not, as the title-page is out.

"*Monday, December 11th.*—Made the land soon after daybreak, and we cast off the *Barque*, and lay-to at 11 A.M.   I went with Webb in the jolly-boat ashore ; he for orders, I to learn news.   Saw Anderson on the wharf—he is looking well—he is Commissary of Ordnance now.   Met Shakespear, and went out to the troop, one and a half mile north-west of Balaklava. Found them admirably situated, as far as protection from the weather is concerned, on a little hill, surrounded by much higher ones—the cavalry close to,

and the French on the heights above us. The roads
dreadful even now—what must they be in wet weather?
Our troop looks much better than I expected—horses
thin and ragged, but not starving; men satisfied, and
not overworked; officers *fat*, and good-humoured!
Returned to the *Curaçoa*, and got my traps on shore."

It is from the journals and letters of others that we
chiefly learn how, as soon as he began to recover from
his own illness, Arthur Vandeleur devoted himself to
reading the Bible, and speaking words of consolation
to the sick and dying men in Scutari Hospital; and in
like manner, when in the Crimea, he was continually
to be found by the side of the wounded, bringing help
and comfort both for body and soul.

CHAPTER XI.

The Siege.

" Few, few shall part where many meet,
The snow shall be their winding-sheet,
And ev'ry turf beneath their feet
Shall be a soldier's sepulchre."

During that terrible time, every fresh account from the Crimea concentrated upon our army all sympathy and thought at home; and numerous were the schemes formed for alleviating sufferings borne by our noble soldiers, with such heroic fortitude as, in the mere retrospect, still sends through our hearts a throb of pain with a thrill of triumph. One day, when a bale of warm clothing and of books was in process of packing at Beckenham Rectory, our ever-welcome and honoured friend, Colonel Anderson, arrived from Woolwich, and inspected the goods with kindly and cheering commendations as to the selection. After noticing parcels of books addressed to friends of ours in several different regiments, " And will you not send some," he asked, " to the Royal Artillery?" On our inquiring to whose care they might be sent, he at once named his young friend, Mr Vandeleur; and, after describing him in language of tender admiration and regard, he added, "And will you write to him, when you send the parcel? He would greatly value a letter from you, and you will find that his is indeed a lovely young spirit to enter into Christian communion with."

From that date commenced a correspondence, which rapidly ripened into a friendship of no ordinary charm and value to me. To him it seemed, as time proved its truth, to answer, in some little measure, the constant yearnings of his orphaned heart for an affection which should recall to him, however faintly, a mother's love and care.

He answered my letter whilst ill of fever in Scutari Hospital; and brightly and warmly grateful was his ready response to it. Often did he refer to it afterwards, as the "morning star of our friendship." But it was not until that last long conversation, already alluded to, which he held with me a few days before his death, that I heard from his own lips that he owed, under the blessing of God, to that letter, his enjoyment of the full liberty of the children of God, the undoubting and abiding assurance of the forgiveness of sins to the believer in Jesus.

Enclosed in that letter was a note of introduction for him to Captain Vicars, 97th Regiment; which he delivered immediately on his return to the Crimea. This introduction resulted in a brief but blessed friendship, ending, in four short months, with Hedley Vicars' death. "Ending!" Oh no, not ending! That which came from Heaven must return thither. Like water, it must find its level. Like the living water, poured from the eternal centre into the mortal heart of man, and springing up again, with that dying life absorbed into it, unto life everlasting. Such Christian friendship as that óf Hedley Vicars and Arthur Vandeleur is immortal likewise.

If our state in this world be but the infancy to the glorious maturity promised us beyond the grave, shall we forget, in the manhood of the soul, the friends of our childhood? Did He who is the type and head of all humanity, who has combined and concentrated in Himself the double nature, the tenderness of the woman with the strength of the man, did He forget His own familiar friends, in His resurrection life?

Had He not a heart for penitent Peter; and an appropriating love for John, from the time of His various appearances after His rising from the dead, to the date of His withdrawing the beloved apostle from the arena of missionary duty to the exile of Patmos, there to reveal Himself to the Seer's enraptured eye?

And was not the consolation given by St Paul to the Thessalonian mourners, weeping over open graves, an assured hope of mutual recognition for renewed and delightful intercourse with their "dead in Christ," in a new and glorified life, when he assured them that they should be "caught up TOGETHER WITH THEM in the clouds, to meet the Lord in the air." Together, and not recognising each other, like friends that meet in mist, and that mist for ever unsunned away! Could the apostle have ventured with such feeble bands to bind up broken hearts—or to offer such a hope as the great message of comfort from Him? For those two noble friends, then, so manly and so tender in heart, so chivalrous in spirit, and so full of Christianity's genial and cheerful love, who first met and parted in the dreary night of war, and starlike threw a light upon its gloom, what a meeting can we imagine !

> "Within a land of pure delight,
> Where saints immortal reign,
> Infinite day excludes the night,
> And pleasures banish pain."

"*Saturday, December* 16*th.*—A dreadful day for the horses ; hail, rain, and snow all the morning, with a bitterly cold wind. Three of our horses died during the night. The men have hard work in clearing the mud away. Had stones put in front of the horses to put the hay on, and others to keep the saddles out of the mud. Ordered No. 1 to close in their horses to the centre after grooming them, to give them the benefit of mutual heat and some little shelter. The roads are covered with dead horses, mules, and bullocks."

"*Tuesday, December* 19*th.*—The long-expected mail has arrived, bringing me several most welcome letters. Fifteen suits of warm clothing for the horses received ; also bales of blankets, and the clothing for the men due next April. Old England is at last roused to a sense of our misfortunes, and is determined to atone for her dilatoriness by her liberality."

"*Saturday, December 23rd.*—Rode the Czar to the front to see Colonel Dacres, Captain Vicars, 97th, and Willy Anderson. I saw Captain Vicars, and we talked a long time together; poor fellows they are dreadfully uncomfortable. His bed consists of a few bushes laid on large stones. He says two hundred of the men of his regiment have to go daily into the trenches. They have also to find out-lying pickets and three regimental guards. So the men are sometimes on duty thirty-six out of forty-eight hours—too much, this! They have great difficulty in getting anything brought up for them from Balaklava. Found it very cold; my fur coat and long boots hardly kept the piercing wind out. Thank God that I have them!

"*Sunday, December 24th.*—This afternoon the thermometer sank almost to freezing point, and in the evening all the tents began to freeze. (10 P.M.) Thornton has just called out to me to say that the inside of his tent is all bespangled with icicles. Mine is not so for I have a little charcoal burner with a few embers still alight in it. We had no service to-day, the weather and duty preventing it. Thornton always reads it in the hospital on Sunday. The poor fellows there were so glad to get the little books dear Colonel Anderson sent me. Little books are much more readily received than tracts, for a careless soldier hates the name of tract. I have also lent them several of my own books."

"*Monday, December 25th.*—Another Christmas-day. How different in every respect from those happy Christmas days I have spent in Old Ireland.

"*Tuesday, December 26th.*—Got on well with our stabling to-day, and put in twenty horses. Commenced digging a hole for my hut; it is to be very small, as I shall probably not be with the troop long—nine feet by seven—just room for my bedstead and a fire-place. The clay is very suitable for the purpose. I saw my name in the *Gazette* to-night as Captain, *Times* 9th December; *Gazette* 4th."

"*Thursday, December 28th.*—Went into Balaklava to see Anderson, having received a note from him last night. It turned out that he had recommended me to Colonel Morris, 1st Division, as his adjutant. I wrote and applied for the post, and have got it. For this piece of good fortune, I have, under God, to thank my dear kind friend Anderson, who exerted himself strongly in my favour.

"*Friday, December 29th.*—Went up to see Colonel Dacres about my appointment; he had no objection, and at once asked Lord Raglan if he might give me the appointment. His Lordship consented, and called me up, and spoke to me: he asked about Maude, and expressed his regret at losing him from the army."

"*Sunday, December 31st.*—On awaking found the ground covered with snow—cold and frosty. Thermometer in my tent 34°. Great discomfort—everything

upside down in my tent. No servants—no mess. Breakfasted with Woodhouse and Co. Went to church a.
eleven, with the 1st Division, viz. Guards and 97th Regiment—Litany and sermon. Mr Jackson, late a missionary, preached; very short sermon, but very good one, all
to the point; subject, "This do in remembrance of me,"
Luke xxii. 19; chiefly drawing our attention to the
fact of this being a command, not a permission only,
and that he did not wish to see officers only, when the
sacrament should for the future be administered, but
soldiers too. He gave notice that every Sabbath afternoon at three, it would be administered in his tent: and
(which I like much) he invited every soldier to come
and speak to him at any hour he liked. He is a worthy
successor of that good man, Mr Halpin."

"*Tuesday, January 2nd.*—The Russians fired last
night with cannon on our advanced pickets from
Inkerman valley. Am in a greater state of discomfort
than I have been since I left England. The interior of
my tent is quite a slough, the rain having dribbled in
under the door during the night. Have neither servant
nor groom,—our horses, too, got no hay to-day, there
being none at Balaklava; owing, I have no doubt, to
further mismanagement. Rained unceasingly. Trying
to dry my famous Russian leather boots, burned the
front out of one of them. Great misfortune this. *On
dit*, Prince Menschikoff says he has three generals of
great renown coming to his assistance, which the allies

know nothing about, viz. January, February, and March !!! I imagine there is some truth in the statement, whether he ever said so or not."

"*Thursday, January 4th.*—My poor horses suffer dreadfully. The horse clothing was all frozen over them to-day when I first saw them. Have had no hay for two days. I give them a little biscuit, which they devour ravenously."

"*Saturday, January 6th.*—Went down into the trenches to-day with Colonel Morris and Maxwell. Entered the 21-gun battery, which is on the crest of a hill, about a mile in advance of the Light Division picket-house. The Woronzoff road passes close by this house, and leads down near the battery. The snow lay on the ground a foot thick in many places; but notwithstanding this, we could see thousands of shot strewing the ground. When we got near the battery there was hardly a square yard without one or two 30-pounders, or 40-pounders. I can only compare its appearance with that of a turnip field with the turnip-tops eaten off. It is hardly credible that the Russians could have fired so many shot and shell at us, and yet have done so little damage. A naval officer said, that in one place, five yards by one, he counted 250, and even then left off before he had reckoned them all.

"It was on this road that Richards and Maxwell had, on two or three occasions, *in open daylight*, to take down five or six waggons together, loaded with powder. A pleasant position, truly, to ride close to five tons of powder, exposed to a storm of shot and shell from thirty heavy guns. Every shot which missed our battery came up close to them, and each had a marvellous escape. On one occasion, a shell stuck in the nave of one of the wheels when Richards was in charge. He imagined it was a shot, and went up to it; when close he saw the smoke, and instantly threw himself on his back; at that moment the shell burst, blew the wheel to pieces, and a fragment passed close over his body. Every one here testifies to Maxwell's coolness under fire."

"*Sunday, January 14th.*—No service to-day on account of the snow. It is now so deep (20 inches) on the ground as to make it almost impossible to get firewood. Even the little branches which used to indicate the proper place to dig, are now covered. To-day the wind was very high and cold, and the drift so great as to make it most unpleasant travelling. We expected to have no dinner to-day from want of fuel, however we managed at last to get some, and had an excellent dinner. No one would believe (except those who have lived the same kind of life as we now are doing) how our spirits rise and fall in almost exact proportion to the supply of our animal comforts. This, however, is a sad truth, and has a most important bearing on the progress of the war. We expected to have no dinner to-day, and we all (very much in consequence) wrote doleful letters to our friends, and no doubt said the army was suffering extreme hardships. The staff, I have no doubt, wrote in their private correspondence that the army was hardly suffering at all, because they enjoy every luxury and comfort.

" *Monday, January 15th.*—Weather still cold, and blowing hard. Nothing important doing. Yesterday afternoon went over to see Vicars, 97th, and found that he has had a second escape from his charcoal stove. Thank God he is still alive, and tolerably well. With what signal manifestations of mercy and love the Lord our God preserves His own. Had some conversation with him on the subject of a prayer-meeting, which I think it would be so desirable to establish in the Division. Graydon, Vicars, Major Ingram, 97th, W. Anderson, and myself, might very well form such, and we are all within a few hundred yards, except W. Anderson. Who can tell the amount of benefit our souls might receive were we thus to meet for mutual edification, and prayer, and studying the Word of God. May He bless our efforts!"

" CAMP BEFORE SEBASTOPOL, *January 19th,* 1855.

"MY DEAR COLONEL,—Having been in a state of uncertainty and extreme discomfort the last three weeks, I have hitherto been unable to comply with your very kind request, that I should write frequently to you. The thermometer indicating cold of 7° or

8° in my tent, the floor of which consisted chiefly
of frozen mud, you can imagine such a state of
things was not calculated to induce me to sit down
quietly for the purpose of transferring my thoughts to
paper. Having, however, yesterday had the pleasure
of seeing your dear son William at Inkerman, I can
no longer forbear giving you the pleasure, which I
know you will feel, when I tell you he was then quite
well and very cheerful. . . . . He has managed to
make himself tolerably comfortable, and though so
great a distance from Balaklava, tells me they are well
supplied with rations. . . . . His brother John watches
over him just like a father, and is continually sending
him up comforts of one kind or another ; there never
was a more affectionate brother in the whole world.
Indeed, my dear Colonel, I have good cause to speak
of your son in terms of warm gratitude ; for he has
obtained for me the appointment which I now hold,
that of Adjutant to Colonel Morris, commanding Royal
Artillery, 1st Division, and this without any suggestion
on my part. He kindly obtained the promise from
Colonel Morris ; and in consequence of his recommendation alone, Colonel Morris acceded to my request.
This is thus the second appointment which I have
obtained through you and your family. . . . . John,
when I saw him last, some days ago, was quite well,
and fully employed as usual. I suppose he will get
one of the packets that are going, and hope so for his

sake, he is so anxious to get home. This, by the by, is the great failing with all the married men ! . . . . Concerning the state of affairs out here, there is little worth mentioning, which the newspapers do not give in full; their accounts, especially those in the *Times*, are, I regret to say, only too true. . . . . However, thank God, we have, I think, seen the worst, and are now improving much—I trust permanently. The severe frost has at last given way, and a steady thaw set in, with a S.S.E. wind, and we all rejoice in the probability of its continuance. The greater part, too, of the warm clothing, of which there is a most abundant supply, has been received and distributed, much to the benefit and comfort of the whole army. . . . . We have now hardly any chaplains with the army. Mr Watson has arrived, and is at Balaklava with the Highland Brigade; I trust his health will enable him to remain. When I next go to Balaklava, I purpose calling on him. After your account of him, I am sure I should enjoy his society very much, and shall try to know him intimately; there are so few out here with whom I can converse on these subjects, which I can truly say, notwithstanding all our bustle, excitement, and annoyance, are still dearest to me. With Captain Vicars, 97th, I had the other day some sweet communion. He is indeed, 'a man of God.' I hope to see much of him.

"Willy, to my great delight, has promised to come

and spend a few hours with me on Sunday next, and I hope Vicars will come too. Surely these are times when we ought to think much of another and a better world. Ever your affectionate and obliged

"ARTHUR VANDELEUR."

"*Sunday, January 21st.*—My birthday—twenty-six years old. How many mercies have surrounded me during the past year; may my life, as well as my lips, shew forth my gratitude! No Division church-parade; so Wodehouse read the service to his company. Poor fellows in hospital very glad to get some books;—may the Lord impress the great truths contained in them on their hearts. They were also glad to have service read to them in the evening;—hope I shall be able to continue this. Went over to see Vicars, 97th—had some conversation with him and Major Ingram—purpose going over to see them often. It is very sweet to have some one within reach with whom I can commune on sacred subjects. Here trifling, chaffing, and noisy conversation, engross the whole of our evenings, except that time which is occupied with whist, to the exclusion of anything sensible, charitable, or refined. I wish I had my dear friend Bruce out here; but I must not be selfish, and wish my dearest friend to come out to such a life as we now have—one of hardship, annoyance, and selfishness; a life to all but a Christian (who can at times abstract himself from all around, and have his mind watered, comforted, and re-strung, by communion with our blessed Redeemer) detrimental to every kindly feeling and noble sympathy. I almost repent of my decision to remain out ;—but no, I will trust my covenant God, and believe that He has great stores of mercy laid up for me ; and that He has a glorious purpose of love with regard to myself and those among whom I am placed. Oh, to honour Him before men !"

"*Sunday, February 4th.*—Read service to men in hospital, and went to Ingram's tent, but they had had their service.

"*Monday, February 5th.*—Lord Rokeby takes command of the Brigade of Guards, 540 bayonets. Commenced my stables, and worked hard myself, sledging and picking. Got one well finished, and put in 'Czar.'"

The following letter was written at this date :—

TO REV. C. FLEURY.

"Camp before Sebastopol,
February 5th, 1855.

"My dear Friend,—It requires a considerable amount of moral courage and perseverance, to accomplish even a single letter, in these cold and dreary regions. But so grateful do I feel for your last kind and most welcome letter, that I cannot suffer this mail to leave without thanking you for it. It is difficult for you to conceive how the scenes and circumstances in the midst of which I am placed, add to the value of letters such as yours; how they are hailed with delight, read, re-read, and pondered upon, with feelings which it is easier to imagine than describe.

"How happy I should be again to find myself in dear old Dublin, where I enjoyed so many delightful privileges; amongst the chief of which I reckon my "sitting" in the Molyneux, and our much-enjoyed and often-remembered evening readings at your house.

"I trust you and all yours continue well, and that your school succeeds. The principle on which you have established it appears a singular one; but if you get the boys young, I see no reason why you should not succeed. All depends on the correct discernment of character; and I know well that the rod is often most unnecessarily and injudiciously applied; that such treatment often ruins delicate and sensitive natures;—and such natures are the most valuable, as being generally found allied to a high degree of intelligence and a high tone of moral feeling, which, if properly nurtured and delicately handled, might prove a blessing to all with whom they are afterwards thrown, when life's hard toils begin. So, they might be an honour, instead of a disgrace, to the instructors of their youth.

"I imagine that one of the greatest errors committed by many, is the leaving boys quite to themselves during the hours of play, when the rougher natures and the older boys soon get the upper hand, and (unless unusually generous) use their authority only to crush the weakest. I had a long experience of the effect of such conduct, when preparing for the army. This it is that constitutes the great difference between school and home, where the boys are not under strong constraint, and yet never left quite alone.

"How many, many mercies I have experienced from Him whom I do indeed regard as the great Captain of my salvation! Amongst them are the wonderful manner in which I have been preserved in the day of battle, and the health and strength which I now enjoy. Oh that both these and all else that belongs to me might be more and better used for His honour and glory! I find these lines peculiarly applicable to me just now: I have been given to feel something of their truth, depth, and comfort:—

> Know, my soul, thy full salvation;
>   Rise o'er sin and fear and care;
> *Joy to find in every station*
>   *Something still* to *do* and *bear.*
> Think what Spirit dwells within thee!
>   Think what Father's smiles are thine!
> Think that Jesus died to save thee!
>   Child of *Heaven,* canst thou repine?'

"To all, this is a life of trial and hardship, in some sense or other; 'but there remaineth a rest to the people of God.' May we not come short of it! May we work while it is day, and work for God and for our

fellow-creatures. . . . Oh for a speedy end to this war !
Oh that the Prince of Peace may soon restore to us the
blessings of peace !   I think we should know how to
appreciate it now."

" *Wednesday, February 7th.*—Weather still delightful.   Still at work at the stables.   Read much to-day.

" *Thursday, February 8th.*—Had pistol practice
to-day with Pennycuick and Harply.   The arming of
the Inkerman batteries commenced this evening—is
chiefly done by the French—we furnish wheelers.
Took up three mortars and beds.

" *Friday, February 9th.*—Two more new batteries
are to be constructed ; one of nine guns, close to our
advanced trenches in front of Gordon's battery, and
one of fifteen, on the inner slope of the Inkerman hill;
both to fire on the Round Tower; under cover of
which fire an advance is to be made on a hill only 700
yards off from this tower, which commands it ; where
a sand-bag battery is to be erected in one night for
fifteen guns.   A strong sortie will of course be made
on this, which we are to beat back, and entering
pell-mell with the enemy, are to take possession of the
works around the tower and keep them.   How well
this reads—may it be successful in stern reality !

" This is a most memorable day for me.   A good
hope granted of a blessed answer to the prayer of
many years.   New and greater mercies than ever

have been lavished upon me before, by my all-merciful God. Glory, glory, glory, be to His most holy Name for ever! How true are His words, 'Let the hearts of them rejoice, that seek the Lord!'

"*Saturday, February* 10*th.*—One of the most severe days we have had during the whole winter. A strong wind from the N. by W., with sleet and snow. Very trying it must be for the poor fellows in the trenches. Remained at home writing and reading all day.

"*Sunday, February* 11*th.*—Weather too unsettled for church-parade. Read to men in hospital, and wrote in the afternoon."

"*Tuesday, February* 13*th.*—This evening we break ground in advance of Gordon's battery, for a new battery, about 300 yards to the right front of Gordon's. The firing has been very heavy and constant this evening; so I dare say they have already commenced to break the ground. Got hold of a most valuable little book, called 'Spring's Fragments,' this evening, and read the chapter on 'a useful Christian.' Very truthful and forcible. I *must* be a useful Christian, must try to give up my lazy habits, and become much more useful in my generation than I have ever yet been. I cannot do this of myself, but I look to God—the loving God—to strengthen and support me in my determination. Christian knowledge, activity and energy, zeal tempered with discretion, ardent uniform piety, earnest prayer, mortification of an aspiring spirit, the absence of an earthly mind, and great consistency of character; these are some of the requisite graces; and O heavenly Father, for the sake of Jesus Christ, grant them to me, and may all Thy dealings with me be sanctified and made to conspire to this great end!

" *Wednesday, February* 14*th.*—Another lovely day, just like May in England. Thermometer 55°. The French (200 Zouaves) commenced their battery on the right front of Gordon's last night, and it looked very respectable to-day from a distance. In the afternoon, went with W. Anderson over to the 97th camp, where I enjoyed the inestimable privilege of joining with a chosen few in the worship of God in a tent. Ingram read prayers, and Vicars read a sermon. There were also present, Cay, Coldstream Guards; Smith, 97th; Le Couteur, Coldstream Guards; Anderson and myself. We all enjoyed it much."

TO REV. G. DESPARD.

"Camp before Sebastopol, *March 2nd*, 1855.

" My dear George,—You must have often thought, 'What can prevent Arthur from answering my last letter?' That letter, so kind, so interesting, so full of details, was, I assure you, most welcome. I received it just after the skirmish of the Bulgarnac, the day before the battle of the Alma. It was almost the first spare moment I had had since landing, and, lying full length on the ground, dead tired and very hot, I read your letter;

so you see you did not make a bad guess as to the circumstances in which it would find me. How applicable did I then find its concluding passages to be. The Lord our God had then, for the first time, (blessed be His Holy Name!) 'covered my head in the day of battle.' My dear George, though I have never since written to you, I did, I assure you, feel most grateful for your kind wishes and earnest prayers on my behalf.

"As regards myself, I have little of interest to communicate. I was for six weeks sick at Scutari; but, thank God, I got better under excellent medical treatment, and was able to leave that horrible place and return to my duty. Shortly after my return I was promoted, and fell to a company at Corfu. I was very sorry indeed to leave my old troop, to which I was proud to belong. But preferring to remain and see the campaign out, I succeeded in getting the Adjutancy of the 1st Division Royal Artillery, and have been consequently, since the beginning of the new year, encamped on these heights. While down at Balaklava, our hardships were nothing to speak of; but it has been very different since we came up here. Personally, I have not suffered, beyond being sometimes rather short of food, and feeling the cold to be very severe. But I have seen suffering, misery, and death in almost every form, and to a vast amount; and arising, too, I regret to say, chiefly from mismanagement and want of thought. I have myself seen the horses eating the clothing off their own backs to satisfy the cravings of hunger, and whole blankets have been devoured in one night. . . . . Large reinforcements of artillery are daily arriving, and more have been sent for to the Mediterranean stations ; and when they arrive, we shall, I think, be able to commence our fire. . . . . The Russians have now got twenty-two guns in their new work, and we have to throw up two batteries of fifteen guns each to oppose it. But anything is better than inaction. We are all anxious to commence. I humbly trust and pray that we may be wise now, and look for strength and support to the Lord God of hosts. My great confidence is in the prayers that are daily offered up for our success. Ever your affectionate friend, ARTHUR VANDELEUR."

" *Tuesday, March 13th.*—Went down to the Tcher-naya to cut sticks, gather violets, and make a sketch,—all of which I accomplished. It is a most lovely spot. I wish I could do justice to it. The underground town of Inkerman was built, I hear, by the Arians, in the third or fourth centuries, to escape persecution.

" *Wednesday, March 14th.*—Rode with Ingram, 97th, to the Monastery of St George—had a fine day, and enjoyed our ride excessively. We rode round by some of the cliffs, and were much struck with their beauty and arrangement. They resemble the cliffs of Moher on a much smaller scale. After I returned I walked up to the Victoria Redoubt to see the French work.

They are now about fourteen hundred yards in advance of the redoubt, and only eight hundred from the Mamelon, which they are approaching by sap. At seven o'clock we were surprised by hearing the musketry become very sharp, and presently the great guns on both sides joined in, and the firing all round became general, but strongest in front of the Victoria Redoubt; it lasted nearly an hour, when there was a lull of half-an-hour's duration; and then they again began to fire, and the engagement became sharper than ever; it lasted upwards of another hour, and then ceased. It has been, I imagine, a Russian sortie, in force on the new French Parallel. The whole of the French Divisions near this have turned out, and marched up with their artillery. Our Light Division also marched up the hill, and the Siege Train Companies fell in. We remained quiet, knowing we should not be wanted. After two hours' fighting, all is over. Many poor fellows, I fear, lie weltering in their blood now, and why am I spared? Great is the mercy of my good God to me. Last evening, at 5 P.M., one of my dear friends, Captain Craigie, Royal Engineers, was killed by the splinter of a shell, as he was returning from his work; it struck him in the side, and entered his heart—death was instantaneous. Poor dear fellow, his loss is much felt in every way, both in his profession, of which he was an active and zealous member, and in private life, being a most kind and affectionate friend, always full of good humour and fun, and a sincere Christian."

"CAMP BEFORE SEBASTOPOL, *March 16th*, 1855.

"MY DEAR COLONEL,—Shortly after I had written my last letter, I heard of your re-appointment to the Horse Brigade, and in its highest rank. Truly delighted was I to hear that you had rejoined your old and favourite branch of the regiment. I can quite imagine the feeling of legitimate pride and joy with which dear Mrs Anderson must have regarded you, when you had resumed the dress which *she knows* always becomes you so well. John, too, I had much pleasure in congratulating on the birth of the son and heir.

"I often go into Balaklava on foraging expeditions and have always the pleasure of a little chat with John, and I am often privileged with a peep of some of your letters. He is, like most of us, very anxious to get home; and I hope his wish may shortly be gratified, as I, along with all his friends, think he is fairly entitled to some good appointment at home, or even to the great aim of his ambition, a troop. I know well that all his superiors, (and they alone are fit to judge,) consider that he has effected the laborious work of superintending the disembarkation and transmission of the vast amount of gun, shot, and material required for this siege, with energy, ability, and success. The Lord

God has made all that he has undertaken to prosper, and has fulfilled many of the precious promises contained in His Word to him, because he puts his trust in Him. . . . .

"For the last few Sabbaths, we have enjoyed the inestimable privilege of joining with Major Ingram and Captain Vicars, 97th Regiment, Dr Cay of the Coldstream Guards, and one or two other of God's dear children, to worship Him in Captain Vicars' tent. We read the Evening Service and a sermon. You can well imagine how great is the pleasure, how lasting the benefit, which we derive from this sacred employment. For my own part, I can truly say, that these moments are among the happiest and most unalloyed which I have spent since I have been in the Crimea. We are all within a convenient distance of each other; and I sincerely hope we shall be able to continue these meetings, which remind me always of those I so often had the delight of joining in at your house. Poor Captain Craigie, R. E., was with us last Sunday but one; he is now, I feel sure, in the land 'where the wicked cease from troubling, and where the weary are at rest.' He met his death on Wednesday evening, on returning from the trenches. A fragment of a shell which burst a hundred and fifty yards from him, struck him on the left side, and is supposed to have entered his heart. Death was instantaneous. Poor fellow ! there are few who make themselves so universally respected as he did, or so beloved for his temper and good-humour at all times. He is a great loss.....

"We all desire peace, but without Sebastopol, it is out of the question. May the Lord God be with us and prosper us. I have hope now. The 21st inst. has been appointed as a day of humiliation at home. Many praying souls in this army will join you, and I am sure we shall be heard. Please give my kind love to all your family, and Christian regards to B——. Ever your deeply - indebted and affectionate young friend, A. VANDELEUR."

Captain Vandeleur's Journal has copious details of the action of the night of the 22nd of March; which he terms "a glorious affair."

This passage is not inserted here; having been published, in substance, in the Memorials of Captain Vicars. He thus concludes:—

"My dear, noble Vicars! valued friend! there were few like him out here. Cheerful, gentle, unassuming, his society was enjoyed by all who knew him. Warm-hearted, affectionate, and honest, he was valued by those whom he made his friends. Brave, conscientious, kind and considerate in the discharge of his duty; he was respected by his superiors, loved by his inferiors, and deeply lamented by all. A God-fearing, righteous man, he has, I fully believe, been removed from the evil to come, and is now amid angels and archangels, praising Him who bought him with His blood, before the throne of God and of the Lamb. How little we thought when the very day before, we heard him read the beautiful Church service with the deepest solemnity, that so soon he should be taken from the midst of us. He could ill be spared, as praying souls are but few among us ; and his *was* a noble work amongst the sick and wounded."

"*Saturday, March* 24*th.*—A suspension of hostilities took place to-day for two hours to bury the dead. Great numbers of our officers took the opportunity to go out in front of the French trenches, and see or talk to the Russian officers. I could not go, for I was anxious to get over my work, in order to be able to attend the funeral of my dear and lamented friend Vicars. Some of our officers walked over the grounds almost as far as the Mamelon. Many of the Russian officers spoke English and most of them French, so great chaff went on between us and them."

"*Monday, April* 2*nd.*—No opening to day. Rode with Ingram to the Monastery and made a sketch of that lovely spot.

"*Tuesday, April* 3*rd.*—Paid a round of visits to my friends. Saw Bambrigge of the Royal Engineers, who has lately returned from Ceylon. He goes into the trenches this evening.

"*Wednesday, April* 4*th.*—The first thing I heard to-day was the death of poor Bambrigge, who was killed by a shell from a mortar in our advanced sap last night. He saw it coming, and generously got all the men inside the work; he was last, and the shell fell close to him, and blew him literally to atoms. Poor fellow, he was a contemporary of mine, and a great friend; a very talented officer."

"*Sunday, April 8th.* — Easter-day. Enjoyed the inestimable privilege of partaking of the holy Communion in the school-room, 77th Regiment. Many officers attended, and I enjoyed it exceedingly. May I ever esteem and prize the opportunities which may be afforded me of growing in grace and love. We were under orders to turn out, and march to Balaklava, with four guns from each battery, if there should be an alarm during the night, as Lord Raglan expected an attack —but none came off."

"*Saturday, April 14th.*—A general assault has, it is said, been fixed for this evening, or rather just before daylight to-morrow morning. The French to attack the Round Tower, or Mamelon, Flagstaff Battery, and Quarantine Fort; while we are to go in at the Redan and Barrack Battery. Firing kept up very brisk. We opened the eight-gun battery on the right yesterday, with excellent effect, and the six-gun battery on the left, which was, however, soon shut up; the Russians brought such a number of guns to bear on it, four guns were disabled out of five—a sergeant and seven men killed in half-an-hour. So much for our advanced batteries. Captain Oldershaw was almost the only man unwounded, when he shut up the embrasure and marched the remnant of his detachment off.

"*Sunday, April 15th.*—No assault; firing continued.

"*Monday, April 16th.*—Firing still kept up, but weaker.

"*Tuesday, April 17th.*—Firing ordered to be reduced; and so the second siege is virtually terminated!"

CHAPTER XII.

Hopes Fulfilled.

"When I His yoke do bear,
And seek my chiefest joy
But in His righteousness, and sweet employ,
He maketh me His care;
Early and late doth bless,
And crowneth work and purpose with success."

"Steamer 'Canadian,' off Constantinople,
May 4th, 1855.

"My dear Colonel,—You will doubtless be surprised when you read the above address. I must explain that having been laid up for ten days with an attack of low fever during the latter part of our second—and, I regret to say, fruitless—bombardment, I was ordered a month's sick leave to Constantinople to recruit: but just at this time my chief, Colonel Morris, applied for leave on private affairs to England, and obtained it to the end of July, ... and I join my company at Corfu. I am now on my way thither in this magnificent vessel, which sailed from Balaklava on the 2nd. She goes direct to Corfu to bring up a regiment. We stop only a few hours at Constantinople. I cannot tell you how happy I am to get away from the scene of strife and carnage, and again to become a quiet member of society. Many causes have conspired to bring about this change of feeling in me, which I can better explain when I have the pleasure of seeing you. This,

I trust and expect, please God, is not very far distant, as I purpose applying for leave to England immediately on my arrival at Corfu. . . . .

"What a pleasure it will be again to enjoy the society of my excellent and valued friend Bruce. It is a most cheering prospect to me. I left dear John two days since: he accompanied me on board. How the dear fellow longs to be in England: though labouring energetically and very successfully here, his heart is with you all at home. . . . .

"A secret expedition sailed yesterday, (3rd,) as is supposed, to take Kertch, and force a passage into the Sea of Azoff. It consisted of the 71st, 93rd, 42nd, and 43rd Regiments, and Barker's Battery, with all the small steamers and gun-boats—the land forces under the command of Colonel Cameron. I am glad of this, as the variety will rouse up the spirits of our troops, who are only anxious to get at their foe on something like fair terms. The English spirit of perseverance is now thoroughly aroused. . . . . Out here we want a man accustomed to success even in small affairs, and one who knows the value of TIME. Napoleon said once, 'These Austrians are not accustomed to estimate the importance of MINUTES in war, but I know their value.' The Russian general, no doubt says, 'These English don't know the value of weeks or even of months!' Ever your affectionate young friend,

"A. VANDELEUR."

On the 25th of May, he landed in England; and in the course of a week from that time, paid his first visit to Beckenham Rectory. A beginning was then made of frank and frequent intercourse, and of delightful friendship, which during the five following years struck its roots deeper and firmer, and grew and blossomed unchecked and unchilled; culminating only as to its earthly existence, with his withdrawal from our sight, into the "general assembly and church of the firstborn."

It would not be easy to give an idea of the charm of living sunshine which seemed to radiate about him; uniting, as he did, the most polished manners with the frank simplicity of a high-hearted, eager boy; mellowing and merging both in the tender glow of "love to the brethren," which overflowed a heart in which his Saviour's love was "a spring, whose waters failed not;" few could meet him without being conscious of an atmosphere of light, warmth, and freshness diffused around.

From that time, no joy of ours was unshared with him. And never did he hear of illness in our home or anxiety in our hearts, without riding over from Woolwich at the earliest time he could command, to comfort us with his most understanding sympathy, and to strengthen us with his prayers.

During the summer and autumn after his return, he

frequently accompanied us on our visits to the navvies
and other workmen, then applying for admission to the
Army Works Corps, who assembled daily for hours in
the grounds of the Crystal Palace; and once was able
to go with my sister and myself to Greenhithe, for one
of our farewell interviews with these men, on board the
ships sailing for the Crimea. The manly simplicity,
clearness, and vigour of his addresses to them, and
the fervour of his prayers, were long remembered by
those who heard them.

The impression which his brave and blameless character produced upon young men of his own position
in life, may be gathered from the following sketch
of his character, by a member of our family-circle, who
was at that time at home whilst awaiting his commission; and who was regarded by Arthur with great and
increasing affection from their first acquaintance:—

"You have asked me to give you my impressions of
dear Arthur Vandeleur, and I must thank you for thus
putting it in my mind to look upon the pattern which
he has left. For it is always an edifying work, as well
as a labour of love, to think upon the finished course
of those, who through faith and patience, inherit the
promises.

"It is only impressions, indeed, that I can give you;
for though I saw him often during the five last years

of his life, yet it was only for a little while at a time. I never was so fortunate as to live with him. I only had passing glimpses of the fair stream of that pleasant life.

"But I will try and recall what I thought of him, the first time I saw him ; my first impression of him ;—I like that word as applied to him, because nobody could see him without being impressed by him ;—his manner, his voice, his face, all impressed you.

"His manners were those of a thorough gentleman, and something more. Your true English gentleman is not a man to be liked very much at first sight; there is too little geniality about him for that. But you liked Vandeleur at once, because you felt as if he liked you.

"There was a frank openness and a readiness 'to be friends,' that was very engaging.

"His was one of those clear ringing voices, that remind one of distant bells. His face was altogether an uncommon one. It was handsome, manly, expressive, and even more than all these. It seemed to me, beyond any other man's, to deserve the epithet of 'beautiful.'

"The high colouring of the cheeks, although it told the sad story of a setting sun, added to the beauty of the face in repose. It was when thus quiescent in thought, that his countenance made the greatest impression upon me.

"At such times the deep, quiet look of that liquid

blue eye used to seem to me to be beaming with high hope, or rather with a high resolve.

"And later, towards the close of his life, all could see in that clear, earnest gaze, that he carried this banner through the field of life: 'I believe in God the Father Almighty.'

"There are men that are flattered, and so there are men that are slandered by their faces. His was not only an expressive face, but it was truly a key to his character, as well as an index to his mind. One could have said from it that his affections were very strong; and though manly and fearless, yet his look had much of woman's gentleness in it. And his *was* a tender manhood. I am inclined to think it was all the greater and braver for being so. Moreover, from his face I should have said that perhaps his feelings were slightly too sensitive for his own comfort in this work-a-day world. I should have imagined, too, that his sense of duty and honour would be very high pitched, and more so than would consort with selfish, worldly wisdom. His mind, too, I think, set its mark upon his features. His talents were rather those of acute observation and delicate perception, than of striking originality, excepting in scientific inventions, in which he excelled. His accurate knowledge of his duties, his love for his profession, his readiness and steadiness, or as we soldiers call it 'smartness,' together with his dashing gallantry, and, no less than these, his cool intrepidity, moral and physical; these things, I say, were well known in that branch of the service to which he belonged ;—that service which of all others makes the greatest calls upon those totally different species of power—patient tenacity and prompt activity. His religion might almost be seen in his face. It was eminently natural religion. I do not mean that much-vaunted, easily-attained, but valueless and powerless thing that men often call 'natural religion ;' nor that simple and sublime creed of a fruitful earth and benignant Providence that St Paul taught the men of Athens, which is the only form of natural religion that has this principle for its essence that 'God is Love.' But I mean rather that his religion was just like himself. You never saw Vandeleur without his religion.

"I have said that I saw him at intervals ; and I must add that each successive meeting shewed me that his light was one 'which shineth more and more unto the perfect day.' His was Christianity hopeful and happy, advocated in words, recommended by practice, accepted in heart, adorned in life, triumphant in death, and, thanks be unto God, now perfected in glory. How good and pleasant a thing it is in thought to follow such a one as he 'went up through the regions of the air,'—'being swallowed up with the sight of angels, and with hearing of their melodious notes, on within the gate of the city.' And how fully one can enter into those two sentences, which to my mind express most truly the feelings of the Christian as he thus lingers on the threshold just crossed by a departed brother. The one, John Bunyan's, when he tells of Christian's entrance into glory, 'which, when I had seen, I wished myself among them.' The other, the language of our Church, when, after praying for all members of Christ's Church militant here on earth, she recalls with fond remembrance and triumphant thankfulness, those who have fought the fight, and kept the faith, and finished their course with joy, and says, 'We also bless Thy holy Name for all thy servants departed this life in thy faith and fear.'

"Surely these two thoughts—the longing to follow where they have entered in, and the deep sense of thankfulness that they have been kept by the power of God through faith unto salvation—are those most befitting the Christian, when he thinks of one 'who all his weary length of life has trod,' and is now 'a pillar within the temple of his God.'"

Shortly after Arthur Vandeleur's return home, he went to Ireland, and spent some time with his friends at Kiltanon. He returned to England, brilliant with joy in the realisation of the hope which had been his cherished dream from boyhood. A dream cherished alike through sunshine and shade, in presence and hope, in silence, absence, and hopelessness, by the unwavering truth of that steadfast heart. God be praised for the four bright years of married happiness which crowned his faithful love !

Somewhat of a little chart of his heart and life during the remainder of the year may be seen in the following letters :—

"KILTANON, *June 18th*, 1855.

"I grieve to think that my silence should have caused you anxiety as to my voyage, &c. How unworthy I am of such kind and tender care. Your long letter gave me the greatest pleasure.

"I forgot to enclose Duncan Matheson's letter in my last. I rejoice to know that his health is sufficiently restored to enable him to resume that most glorious work of winning souls to Christ. As I read his letter, I regretted that I had not known more, when in the Crimea, of such a devoted Christian missionary. I am glad to hear the last supply of books which you sent out to my care was not lost by missing me. But (don't think me partial!) I wished that Artillerymen rather than the Highlanders should have benefited by your kindness; for the Highlanders are so well looked after in that way. Mr Matheson speaks of the prevalence of card-playing in the camp. I can confirm his testimony, for I, too, saw much of it. Long have I looked with horror upon this vice of gambling, which engenders selfishness, envy, hatred, and other evil passions. It is a powerful weapon in Satan's hands for ruining souls. Idleness has nourished this vice; and so I trust that a general move of our forces, from the heights more into the interior, will tend to check it, by removing the opportunities afforded by long residence in one spot.

"Will you be so very good as sometimes to let me see your Crimean letters, particularly any from a soldier or a navvy. Their letters are generally so charming. Yesterday, I saw one from a man (a countryman of mine, I need hardly tell you after you have heard the quotation) to his wife; the first half of the letter was written in ink, the last in pencil, 'because a cannon-shot had just come in and knocked over his ink-bottle! and killed four men alongside of him!!'

"I am so glad you hear from Major Ingram. He is a fine fellow; so steady and consistent in his Christian conduct—graces which I so much need. Do, my very dear friend, pray God to give me these, especially. I prize your prayers so much. It seems to me that 'He heareth you always.' Bless you for praying for me.

"Major Ingram and I have several times prayed together in camp. When you write, tell him that I remember him most affectionately.

"I cannot wonder at your faith for answers to prayer for the things of this temporal life, being shaken by the death of one so precious and so much prayed for as Hedley Vicars. It *is* hard to understand the wherefore. But as that which you loved best in him was the image of Jesus; as He was 'all in all' even in Hedley Vicars to you; He still remains 'all in all' to you, and to one still more deeply afflicted by this great

loss. . . . . But if it was contrary to some of your
earnest prayers, it was and is in answer to others of
your prayers, perhaps overlooked by you now, but
surely not less earnest, nor less remembered of God.
You asked for spiritual blessings for him almost without measure, and who shall number them now?   And
you asked for the outpouring of the blessed Holy
Spirit upon our soldiers and our sailors, and you are
still imploring the same, with ten thousand others of
Christ's people.   Perhaps God knew that the Memoir
you have been requested to write of our beloved friend,
would be the very thing to promote spiritual life
amongst those whose souls you plead for.   'A real
Christian and a fearless soldier ;—is there in the world
a finer character?' is a question on the lips of many
now.   And Hedley Vicars' Life and Correspondence
will go further towards answering the question whether
the two can be combined, and settling the point on the
side of our God and His Christ, than even the grand
old Life of Colonel Gardiner—at least, so I think.
And I earnestly pray that it may prove to be so.   And
then your hearts will be cheered by the knowledge that
'he, being dead, yet speaketh' to his Master's honour.
Surely this will be a comfort to you—and to her. * * *

"Kiltanon is a delightful spot; one of the most
beautiful places in the country.   I am enjoying the
society of my cousins most entirely.   This is a family
in which I have long found the delights of Christian

intercourse and fellowship. I should be glad if you knew them.

"You asked me to let you know what I was doing at Ralahine. On Saturday, I went over to see my tenants, about ten miles from this place. They were all delighted to see me, and I felt my heart warm towards them as their honest welcome rang in my ears. A better-disposed set of men are not to be found in this country. I was deeply grieved, however, to find my school still unattended, and called them all in there, and earnestly expostulated with them about the neglect of their children, till I actually found myself giving them something like a sermon.

"But I fear, as yet, that all my efforts will be in vain: the priests have too much influence, and have already commenced their persecutions. On Friday, I found that Father —— had held a 'station' at the house of one who seems most to favour my views. (A 'station' is a public meeting.) He made the poor man's wife kneel before him, and then, in the presence of the assembled crowd, refused to give her absolution, unless she would promise never again to admit the school-master to read the Bible to her: she would not promise, and had to rise unabsolved.

"But, with the blessing of God, I will persevere in doing my duty by them; and I have a strong hope that our efforts will one day be crowned with success, as their eyes are being gradually opened, and many of them continue to read the Word of God, notwithstanding the denunciation of Father ——. Pray for them sometimes, will you? Give them a corner in your heart, with the five hundred navvies just sailing for the Crimea."

"*July 5th.*—The very day I wrote to you last, I received a letter informing me of my appointment to the Arsenal (as Captain Instructor) being sanctioned, and requiring my immediate presence at Woolwich. Of course, I set off the following day. I have, as you may imagine, plenty to do, and am in a very unsettled state, without a house or servants as yet; *but* for all this, I would not have let three days elapse before writing to inform you of my good fortune. I know well from whom this blessing comes, and most truly do I desire to fill my new post entirely to His glory. Most cordially do I join with you in praying that, hour by hour, God the Holy Spirit would give us more of Himself; having Him, we need no more. Oh, how much do we need His enlightening and sanctifying influences in these days of error, of ungodliness. . . . . I had the very great pleasure of meeting dear Mr Chalmers and his pleasant son yesterday evening, at the house of our mutual friend, Colonel Anderson. A most delightful evening we spent, with the 10th of St John for our subject."

". . . . . *July 16th.*—I long to introduce my Mary to you. I know you will keep your promise to love her; and find it easy work, indeed. For twelve years I have loved her, and every successive year more and more, as I saw deeper into her character.

"I am looking for great blessing to us both from your mother-sisterly love and friendship. Yet all earthly love is but a faint reflection of the infinite, everlasting, and most glorious love of our God and Saviour. Oh, to realise the depths of that! We shall know it deeply here, and perfectly hereafter, and in that will be fulness of joy. Ever your son and brother in Christ Jesus our Beloved."

"Royal Artillery Barracks, Woolwich,
Midnight, July 26th.

"I cannot rest without sending a line of thanks to you, for your trusting kindness in allowing me to carry away for a day, that splendid, characteristic letter of him who is still—and for ever—so deservedly loved by you all. It is charming, from beginning to end; but it is in that part of the letter in which he speaks of the separation from sympathising spirits—making the Lord Jesus so precious to his soul, that the force of his religious character, or rather the reality of his faith, comes out. But a short time, comparatively, a soldier of the Cross, how quickly he had passed through all the lower grades, and to what a high position had he attained.

"Independently of the large measure of grace required, before any one could feel that the loss of fellow-ship with Christians increases the enjoyment of fellow-ship with Christ; it also demands a determination of will and mental energy, to overcome the difficulties of such a position ; such as Joshua shewed, when he said, 'As for me, I WILL serve the Lord.'

"I fear I am not nearly so far advanced. In the Crimea, my heart was not so happy, because not so holy, as when I enjoyed more frequently the external means of grace. At times, I *was* permitted to drink deep at the Fountain-head; but I missed the streams sadly. It is only character of the highest order that can thoroughly overcome the force of circumstances. But the promise stands true for the weakest, of over-coming strength from above : '*My grace is sufficient for thee.*' Oh, for a deeper insight into the fulness of grace and weight of glory that is in Christ Jesus, *for us.*

"God for ever bless you ! I am unworthy to be placed (however much smaller the niche) beside that noble Christian, Hedley Vicars, in your 'mother-sisterly' heart ; and yet I believe God has given me a place there, and will keep it for me always. God for ever bless you and yours. Ever your most grateful and affectionate   ARTHUR VANDELEUR."

"ROYAL ARTILLERY BARRACKS, WOOLWICH,
August 22nd.

" Most warmly and sincerely do I sympathise with

N

you in these new trials : but oh ! how much of comfort
is there in the thought that our heavenly Father sepa-
rates us but for a *short* time from those whom He
takes away, and that they are happy in the presence
of the King of kings.   And there is also that still
more precious thought of consolation to those bereaved,
that the void left in a Christian heart when deprived
of a friend most dear, is always filled by Him who
' well deserves the name of Friend,' and whose love
alone is satisfying to an immortal soul.   You have no
doubt often thought deeply on that beautiful passage,
' These are they which came out of great tribulation,
and have washed their robes, and made them white in
the blood of the Lamb,' &c.   Oh, what a world of
meaning and joy to the Christian there is, in the whole
of that passage.   It is not only trouble, but the state
of trouble, ' tribulation,' and not only that, but ' great
tribulation ; ' and yet every one of that countless multitude came safe out of all, preserved by boundless
power and grace.   Oh, that at the cost of any amount
of sorrow or suffering, we may be included among that
multitude of redeemed and sanctified ones."

" August 27th.

" So, many thanks for your two notes.   My spirits
are just like a barometer, easily raised or depressed,
but your dear notes always cause the index to point
very high indeed.

" I hope you found ——— tolerably calm; how I should have liked to hear you speaking words of comfort to her troubled heart. How difficult it is so to do! But I know you take the Saviour's own way, and ' weep with them that weep,' and then point to the unspeakable blessing of a certain and glorious, because Christ-like, resurrection : and that must give comfort.

" I hope, God willing, to go over and see you all tomorrow. Dear Colonel Anderson's absence in Scotland, for a month, sets me free on that evening; but Wednesday evening is devoted to my trumpeters' class, in the Barrack Chapel.

" I have achieved a glorious triumph with the fever tincture : I have made a *Doctor* (!) a convert to its efficacy by personal experience. He has suffered from ague for eighteen months, and is now cured. One bottle effected it. I enclose his letter.

" With very kind love, and a multitude of blessings, ever your deeply-attached son and brother."

" WOOLWICH, *August* 31*st*.

" That I have found a second home, within reach of Woolwich, in 'blessed Beckenham Rectory,' is, I am satisfied, one of the greatest proofs of the mercy and love of my God which could be given me. In the bright future, which I humbly trust, if it be my God's will, is before me, one of my brightest day-dreams of anticipation is, to have you and yours staying with us and blessing us by your society, counsel, and encouragement. I know you will come and make our hearts glad by your presence.

"How truly delightful to me are those few hours which from time to time I can spend at Beckenham. I often wish I could get away at more seasonable hours, but I fear that is impossible without defrauding her Majesty; and, as I 'honour the Queen' with my whole heart, I try to give her the best service I possibly can, by remaining diligently at my post, and working to the best of my ability while I am there.

"I am glad you like my thought about Christian and Faithful, and Christian and Hopeful. Did any ever better deserve the name of 'Faithful' than Hedley Vicars? To me it describes him exactly. Strong in faith, vigorous and unswerving in practice, and devoted to the grand and soul-absorbing idea, 'Christ All in all.' Such was the impression he left upon my mind when we communed together, in camp before Sebastopol. And the simile bears to be drawn out further; he died truly in 'Vanity Fair;' and I verily believe that what was said of the martyrs of old, will be found true of him, 'The blood of the righteous is the seed of the Church.'

"God grant me grace always to be 'looking unto Jesus,' as Hopeful was! How greatly I desire to be able to reckon myself among the diligent of the earth, in the cause of Christ! I am not yet, I fear, though I am constantly aiming at it. May grace, mercy, and peace be multiplied to you and yours, is the prayer of your ever affectionate son and brother,

"ARTHUR VANDELEUR."

"ROYAL ARTILLERY BARRACKS, WOOLWICH,
September 11th, 1855.

"Your precious little note I found awaiting my return from London, yesterday evening. How shall I thank you for it, and for lending me those two invaluable letters; they refreshed and delighted my heart and soul. They do give me an insight into Hedley's noble mind and tender heart. It must be an unspeakable comfort to you all, to know that that heart and soul are now where they long wished to be, and where we *hope* (in its full meaning implying expectation) to meet again, where there shall be no more separation, even in the presence of the God of Love.

'Will he there no fond emotion,
    Thought of early love, retain ?
Or, absorb'd in pure devotion,
    Will no mortal trace remain ?

'Can the grave those ties dissever
    With the very heart-strings twined ?
Must he part, and part for ever,
    With the friends he leaves behind ?

'No, the past he still remembers !
    Faith and Hope, surviving too,
Ever watch those sleeping embers
    Which must rise and live anew.'

"And now I must say 'adieu,' which in its original and full significance comes from my inmost soul."

"*September 5th*, 1855.

"I have been sadly disappointed at not being able to find any leisure time for the last three days, in which to write a few lines to express my heartfelt thanks for your charming little present. Even now I have but a few moments, while the workmen are at dinner; but I can no longer deny myself the pleasure that it always gives me to chat with you on paper. You will be glad to know that this little volume of Sacred Poetry is, and ever will be, one of my greatest treasures. A thousand thanks for it, and still more for all you have written in it. It has long been a favourite book with me, but my former copy was given away, before I went to the Crimea, and has not since been replaced. So this one is doubly welcome, coming from such loved hands. It shall be my constant companion in railway and steamboat—it made a trip with me yesterday to London, and warmed and cheered my heart beyond measure. The hymn which I learned was that delightful one, so full of harmony of heart and sound,

'How sweet is morn's first breeze that strays on the mountain,
And sighs o'er its bosom and murmurs away;
　　*　　*　　*　　*　　*　　*
But sweeter, my God, is Thy voice of compassion,
That soft as the summer-dew falls on the mind.'

You know it, no doubt, and if so, I am sure you will

join with me in loving it. I see you have marked another of my favourites, 'The Reverie.' That one falls in more completely with my mind and feelings than perhaps any other. Every thought it contains I have laid up in my storehouse of wisdom and knowledge. The said storehouse has, however, as yet, few bales of goods! But I rejoice to think that more are being added to it daily, and much through your kindness, several of my best being from Hawker's 'morning portion.'

"It made me quite happy when I read your extract from Jeremy Taylor; it was one of the first extracts I ever made, when I began to think seriously, and act from those solemn thoughts. You could not have chosen a more acceptable passage, particularly when I think of the application you intended to make of it. You are too good and kind to me.

"I rejoice to tell you that the elder of my cousins has been successful, and has obtained a very good place among those who have received provisional commissions. The dear fellow, when, after the examination, I spoke to him earnestly on the importance of at once deciding for Christ, said that, with God's help, he would do so. Blessed be God, I think His grace is deep in that young heart. You must have a long and encouraging talk with him, when I bring him to Beckenham. I am sure you will like him—he is so clever, sensible, and well-informed.

"I am almost bewildered with firing great guns all the morning, and have to be at it again now; so please excuse all blunders; and give my reverential love to your beloved father; and much love to all belonging to him."

"ROYAL ARTILLERY BARRACKS, WOOLWICH,
October 5th, 1855.

".... It is so very good of you to tell me from time to time about the work you are engaged in for our beloved Lord and Master: it has a wonderful influence over my failing energies, and invariably rouses me up (thank God!) to renewed activity. Oh, how precious and delightful is it, to be permitted to speak a word or do the most trifling deed from love and gratitude to Him. How strange, then, that we are not—or rather, that *I* am not—always engaged in this blessed work. I know well how deeply you have enjoyed the calm and precious satisfaction, of soul which Jesus gives to those who, in simple faith, endeavour to work for Him; and, I trust that I am beginning—but, oh, at what a great distance —to follow in the same steps and to drink of the same river of life. What a joy to think, that though our feelings of love wax faint and cold, and even appear to ourselves to die, His love is unchangeable, and shall never cease, either in this world or in the world to come.

"Put me in any garret when I go to you, if your 'sea-villa' is as well filled as Beckenham Rectory. I rather prefer a small room; it makes one feel one's-self of more importance: one is lost in a great space. I should fancy this kind of idea must have been in the minds of the Romans; for, as a nation, they built immense palaces and public halls; but their private dwellings were so small that one wonders how a great Roman senator, with his toga, could ever manage to get into his own house. So you see, if I have a little room, you must allow me to consider myself of some importance, while in it and fast asleep!"

Whilst we were spending a short time by the sea-side, I received a letter from Arthur, alluding to, rather than explaining, some great trouble which had come upon him. This was connected, as I afterwards learned, with those trials of his mother's, of years before, which, in his boyhood, he had vainly sought to induce her to share with him. The whole tone of the letter was so unhappy, that I could not but feel that his mother, or his sister, had she been within reach of him, under such circumstances, would have tried to make a home for him, for a few days' change of scene, and of quiet thought and prayer as to the best course for him to take. Accordingly, I returned at once for a few days to Beckenham Rectory, where some members of my family were remaining, whilst the rest were by the sea-side; and we invited him to join us there.

The calm of a Sabbath in that happy home, and the companionship and counsel of my brother-in-law,* between whom and Arthur Vandeleur there was an affection almost fatherly on the one side, and filial on the other, contributed not a little to soothe and cheer his spirit—a spirit so child-like and buoyant, that when the immediate pressure of a burden was removed, even for a day, it sprang up again as joyously as ever; and his light, pleasant, ringing laugh would rejoice the hearts of those around him.

It was for the little act of friendship just alluded to, that his grateful heart overflowed in the following words :—

"ROYAL ARTILLERY BARRACKS,
October 24th, 1855.

" How shall I thank you as I would, for your true-hearted mother-like kindness and goodness to me ; for the comfort of your prayers and faithful counsel, and for your deep, entire sympathy. Never shall I forget the promptness of that unselfish friendship ; nor the feeling of being a son at home, which came to me with a sight of your kindly face.

"For all this, and for those two strengthening, cheering days at Beckenham, in such a time of need, I bless you now ; and shall be able to thank you better, in the world to which my friendships in that sweet home have drawn me nearer.

* Rev. Frederick Chalmers, Rector of Beckenham.

"God for ever bless you with all the riches of His grace and love in Jesus Christ! Had *He* not revealed Himself to me so graciously during those two ever-to-be-remembered days, my distress of mind would have been great indeed, during the whole of this trial. But since those days, (the Sabbath, especially,) I have utterly trusted Him, that out of this great evil He would bring glory to Himself and good to my soul.

"I intrust to you my warm thanks to dear Mr Chalmers. Gratefully do I prize his kindness, his affection, and his counsel; and feel the value of his sound, clear understanding, and tender sympathy.

"On my return to Woolwich, I referred the matter (as he and I had agreed upon) to three of the most judicious of my brother-officers at Woolwich. And now you will see how satisfactory is their decision upon the subject."

*   *   *   *   *

"Oh! for the spirit of praise and thanksgiving, that I might be able to express in words and acts, the intense gratitude and love which fill my soul, to Him who has turned away His anger from me, and is now beaming forth in all the beauty of His glorious countenance, upon His unworthy servant, from behind the thick thunder-cloud. Surely it becomes me to join heart and soul with the Psalmist, and exclaim, ' *What* shall I render to the Lord for all his kindness towards me?' He will shew me *what*, and how, and where; and will

give me strength to perform my vows. I even now
fancy you sent me the very text suited to me—'Peace,
always, by all means ;' and sent of God, in His, not my
way. I hope to write to dear Mr Chalmers to-morrow,
and tell him all that has happened since we parted.
Pray send him my affectionate love for his great sympathy and kindness. I fear all is not over yet. 'The
Lord is my rock, and my fortress and DELIVERER,' and
out of even that trial, He will bring me safe, if He
suffer me to be led into it. May He do anything that
will bring me closer to Himself, and make me lean
more completely upon Him. . . . . Grace, mercy, and
peace be multiplied unto you—God bless you."

" November 3rd.

" . . . . Surely the great lesson those painful part-
ings are meant to teach, is that we should endeavour
more constantly than we do to realise the presence of
our Great Friend, Counsellor and Brother, from the
fullest enjoyment of whose society no power *need* ever
separate us, no not for one moment ; and whose love
for us is so tender that He is grieved when we forget
or undervalue this promise, 'I will never leave thee, nor
forsake thee.' And then the truth and love of our
covenant God enables us to cast all our care for those
we love upon Him who 'careth for us.' And we *do*
know that the Lord loveth to comfort His people. . . . .
" We had a delightful army prayer-union meeting

at Captain Tilley's house on the 1st, to remember our brothers in the Crimea. Our chapter was Hebrews iv. We had a good deal of conversation on the point as to whether that verse, ' The Word of God is quick and powerful, and sharper than any two-edged sword,' referred to the Bible, or whether the whole passage refers to the Lord Jesus. I should like to know what you think ; and please ask your beloved father, who is wisdom itself.

" And now it is already Sunday morning, so I must close. A thousand thanks for your dear letter of sympathy and congratulation—it is very dear to me. May God the Father, Son, and Holy Ghost bless, preserve, and keep you.

" Royal Artillery Barracks.

" How glad I am that Frederick Chalmers has been appointed to the Rifle-Brigade. It is a charming corps, and bears a noble character, in every way.

" God grant that the career of a soldier may prove to dear Fred. one of honour, prosperity, and joy : and that he may never forget to hold as his guiding principle, the promise of the Lord Jehovah, ' Them that honour Me, I will honour.' May he be led to fix his whole choice *at once* upon God for his Master. It will be easier now than ever again. And the undivided heart, surrendered in youth to the best of Masters, has a double blessing resting upon it in the years of manhood.   May his prayer be '*Unite* my heart to fear Thy name.'

"How truly has it been said, our Divine Redeemer did not say 'Ye must not,' or 'Ye shall not,' but 'Ye CANNOT serve God and Mammon.'

"A whole heart for the Lord Jesus, 'who loved us and gave Himself for us;' and a whole life to follow it, is that which you, and I too, desire for ourselves, and all those dear to us.

"Give my love to Fred., and tell him how glad I am to have him as 'one of us;' though he is not in the branch of the service that I love best.

"Tell him, he *must* get leave to be present at my marriage. I look to him as an important actor on that occasion,—now, I trust, not very far distant.   Oh how can I bless and praise my good God as I would, for all the happiness and blessings which He has rained down upon me."

"ROYAL ARTILLERY BARRACKS, WOOLWICH,
November 28th, 1855.

". . . . Well, I do feel for you, most heartily, in this mysterious loss of two of your manuscript chapters of the Memoir;[*] and at a time when every hour of your day is interrupted by arrivals of the men of the Army Works Corps.   It was a subject worthy of having a good cry over!   But now that is done—

* Of Captain Vicars.

take heart again ! I am looking for very great blessing from our God through that record of His grace
—and especially to see it made useful to many of
our soldiers. Therefore, I pray that nothing may
discourage you from finishing it—and that right
quickly.

"How that humble and holy-hearted Christian will
bless and praise his God, in Heaven, when he learns
(as learn he will, I doubt not) that the simple record of
the grace of Christ, which was so strong in him, is
made use of by the Holy Spirit, to light others on the
way to glory. In a word, to lead them to Jesus, 'the
Way, the Truth, and the Life.' . . . .

"What can it matter to one who is a saint *in
Heaven*, if every thought of his heart were revealed to
an audience, consisting of the whole world on earth, if
the grace of God were to be magnified by it ; and the
salvation which is by faith in Jesus Christ, made more
glorious and precious in the eyes of others.

"Do not fear that it will fail to speak with power to
many a heart, by the blessing of God, if only you will
tell the whole story,—the story of a sinner saved by
grace, who washed his robes and made them white in
the blood of the Lamb ; and who overcame the world,
and sin, and the devil, by the blood of the Lamb, and
the power of His Holy Spirit. And the story of
a man with affection, friendship, and love, warm in his
heart ; a brave, good soldier, too ; and all this simply

and entirely consecrated to the glory of his God and Saviour. . . . .

* * * * *

"Frail, human nature is prone to think of, and look out for, only its own happiness and honour; but whatever we may look for, His glory is the grand result which the Christian's God will manifest unto him; and will train him up to seeking, as his first object. Thank God, both you and I can say, Be it so, O Lord; may we see Thy glory, and delight ourselves in it, and Thy likeness in ourselves and those dear to us; then, indeed, shall we be satisfied.

"Thank you and bless you for your most valued letter. I will say nothing now about its contents; as I must be off in a few minutes to teach my class. . . . . I am hoping to write to dearest Mr Chalmers to thank him for the book he brought over for me yesterday; please give him my most grateful thanks, and tell him I shall enjoy its perusal excessively. May he and you, and I, and all we love, daily know more of the depth of the love which is in the heart of Christ Jesus, our beloved Lord and Master, for us; and may *He now* and ever be our ALL in all things, and in every body.

"How much do we see of *His likeness*, in your most beautiful and venerable father. The atmosphere of love and peace which seems ever around him, is indeed a breath of heaven's own air. God grant he may be long preserved to you, and to the Church of God!"

".... I cannot retire without first sending you a short note, to bless you from mine inmost heart for your most welcome and invaluable letter of advice, and for the precious and beautiful Paragraph Bible, and all that is written inside. It would be quite in vain for me to attempt to express all I feel; but believe me, the remembrance of all you have done for me, and these kindnesses in particular, will remain in my heart as long as life shall last. The Lord reward you for all your prayers for us! My precious Mary and I do fervently desire to live entirely according to the will of God; to be 'not conformed to this world, but to be transformed by the renewing of our mind.' .... There is so much joy and happiness in receiving tokens of friendship and affection, that one would be inclined to doubt the truth of that saying of Holy Writ, 'It is more blessed to give than to receive,' were it not that *giving* is the special property of our God; it is one of His peculiar enjoyments, and He has pronounced it to be even more delightful than that which makes us so happy, receiving and possessing His good gifts.

"The delightful feeling which we have in denying ourselves in any way—to be able to give that which will be valued by a friend, or may relieve the poor, does teach us in some small degree,—but oh, how great the gulf between!—what must be the depth of the blessedness which God feels in giving to *all men* liberally and upbraiding not."

Perhaps few people have a better right to make a little dissertation on the happiness of giving, than Arthur Vandeleur had. He was always on the alert for an excuse for making little gifts to his friends; gifts which seemed to be chosen with a sort of intuition as to that which would afford most pleasure. Birthdays, Christmas-day, New-Year's-day, Midsummer-day, days of parting, and days of meeting; all alike were pressed into this service! And to the needy and destitute, his charity was only bounded by his righteous dread of debt, and desire neither to spend nor to give a single farthing which did not positively belong to him; in order that, like Longfellow's 'Blacksmith,' he might

> "Look the whole world in the face—
> For he owes not any man."

CHAPTER XIII.

Married Life.

"So have I sometimes seen a Christian bear
  A brightness, not of earth, but from above,
  Lighting his countenance with rays of love,
  As he descended from the mount of prayer:
  Benevolence, affection, holy peace,
  Serene and humble trust—a soul at rest,
  A faith establish'd, and a peaceful breast;
  A confidence, a joy, which cannot cease:
  These, these have shed a glory pure and bright
  As that which clad the prophet's face with light!"

On the 3rd of January, 1856, Arthur Vandeleur was married at the parish church of Lee, to Mary, eldest daughter of James Molony, Esq. of Kiltanon.

In addition to the large family circle who were present at this marriage, Mr Molony's hospitality assembled many friends of both his daughter and his son-in-law, who came with more than common gladness in their hearts, to see so steadfast an affection rewarded at last.

It was this which gave a distinctive character to the day ; casting the glow of romance over the commonplace incidents and details of a wedding-party.

Few who were present could forget the fatherly and almost solemn tenderness of General Anderson's words, that day ; nor the half-triumphant note in his voice, as he spoke with thankful confidence and delight, of the character of his young friend, as he had watched its gradual development, from the first day of their acquaintance up to that hour.

In referring to that happy morning, General Anderson now writes :—" Little did I imagine, when we met at

the marriage of my beloved friend, that his earthly
career was to be of so short a duration ; radiant as he
then was with health and strength, and sanctified joy.

"Vandeleur *was* a rich trophy of the grace of God.
He was a most beautiful exemplification of living
Christianity, in a true soldier, and a man of a natur-
ally generous and lovely disposition."

In addition to these strong foundations for happiness
in married life, there was in the character of Arthur
Vandeleur, that crown of a high-toned morality—in
itself one of the marks of a noble manhood—a reverence for woman. "To give honour unto the weaker,"
as well as to give succour and support, was a law of his
strong nature. Combined with a firmness of resolve in
all matters of conscience and duty, which nothing could
shake, was a genial, natural chivalry of character—
ever called into play by the thousand little opportunities, in daily life, for considerate and self-sacrificing
tenderness, to a degree which became so completely a
part of his very existence, that it extended throughout
his dying illness.

The following letter was received from him, about a
week after his marriage :—

"HOTEL MEURICE, PARIS, *January 8th*, 1856.

"Our first day here was a Sabbath, and a very blessed
one we both felt it to be. We went to the English
Chapel, Rue d'Aguesseau, and were delighted to find it

was Sacrament Sunday.   We knelt together at the
table of the Lord, our hearts filled with gratitude, and
our mouths with praise, for the great things our covenant God had done for us.   It was unspeakably precious thus to be able to shew our Lord and Master,
that in the midst of our joy and happiness, we remembered Him and His wondrous love to us, and were determined to devote our married life to His glorious
service.   And He did meet with us, and cause us to
feel with joy that the 'light of the King's countenance' was lifted up upon us."

Our intercourse, during the following year, was so
frequent, that light were the labours of correspondence
on either side.

It was delightful to see him in his own home, and
in his sphere of duty.   To the song of praise and
thanksgiving wherewith he made melody in his heart
to the Lord, his life gave back its faithful echoes.

The service of his heavenly King seemed a refresh-
ment to him, after his regular duties in the Arsenal
had been thoroughly performed; and even his exceeding happiness in his home, wrought no diminution of
his spiritual energies.   "The time is short;"—"Work
while it is day:" were words continually on his lips.

Not only were soldiers cared for, but the souls
of the thousands working in the Arsenal, were also
borne upon his heart.   Books, tracts, and cards of

prayer, were distributed amongst them ; a library was
formed ; and, not satisfied with using only these means
of good, Major Vandeleur* and his friend, Captain Orr,
organised two associations amongst these men, one for
those who worked in the Gun-factories, the other for
those who were employed in the Laboratory, for the
purpose of inducing them each to purchase, at a somewhat reduced cost, a copy of M'Phun's Family Bible,
price thirty shillings.   One shilling a-week was the
average sum subscribed.

On the evenings when the subscriptions were paid,
Arthur and his friend conducted Bible-readings with
the men, commencing and concluding with prayer.   I
have seen them riveted by his words, and still more
by the holy joy which lighted up his countenance, as
he spoke to them of the blessed privilege of the daily
study of the Word of God ; and pointed out some of
its glorious riches and beauty.

"Royal Arsenal, *February 29th*, 1856.

"We did so enjoy seeing you in our little home :
next time you come, you must pay a much longer
visit.   You will rejoice to hear that even your short
sojourn in the Arsenal will, through the blessing of
God, be productive of good to those in it ;—to say
nothing of the words of comfort and advice you spoke

* Arthur Vandeleur was promoted to the Brevet-rank of Major
for his services in the Crimea.

to the poor fellows in Dial Square;—for I have been thinking very seriously over your question, 'Is nothing to be done, to rescue the ten thousand poor fellows at work here, from the hands of Satan?' and I think that one plan which we talked over can be carried out. I mean that relative to the lending library. I am certain that it would be highly valued by the workmen, and might effect much good. I am going to ask Colonel Wilmot to take the matter in hand; and if I succeed in this, you may consider it as settled, for he is always successful! God grant it may be so in this instance!"

"ROYAL ARTILLERY BARRACKS, WOOLWICH.

"I feel happy when I know that you speak to our covenant God about me, whether in prayer or praise, and entreat you to continue to do this, for it does me a world of good, more than I shall ever know in this life. I often remember you and your work for Jesus, when on my knees before the ever-open throne of grace. There is a pleasure in prayer, intercessory prayer, which becomes deeper and truer as it is indulged in the oftener. Oh, to know more of such pleasure!"

The date of the following letter has not been ascertained. In its closing paragraphs, we trace an indication of his earnest love and reverence for the Sabbath. Few persons could more closely follow the injunctions

with respect to it, given in Isaiah lviii. 13 ; or more
freely enjoy the privilege annexed to such obedience,—
"*Then* shalt thou delight thyself in the Lord:"—

"My soul owes you much, very much, and as it
cannot repay you, goes to the living Fountain to ask to
have you rewarded out of the fulness of Christ Jesus
our Lord.   Faithful is He that promiseth, who also
will do it.

"Were you not delighted to see the *Times* yesterday?   How every Christian's heart must bound with
joy, gratitude, and thankfulness, at the information it
contained relative to the Sabbath question.   What a
triumphant majority, 376 to 48!

"The Lord Jehovah has wrought, and they have not
been able to make void His law.   Blessed be His holy
Name for evermore!"

"ROYAL ARSENAL, *September 3rd,* 1857.

"One line to tell you the happy tidings of my precious wife's safety, and that she has a sweet little
daughter.   Oh, how shall I express half the gratitude
and thankfulness that fill my heart towards Him who
is indeed the Giver of all good gifts!   The Lord my
God be praised!   I well know how deeply you and all
your dear family will sympathise in *our joy.*   An
eternity will not be sufficient to shew forth His praise
for all His tender mercy towards us."

"Royal Arsenal, October 12th, 1857.

"We propose to have our darling little child made a member of the visible Church of Christ on earth, on Wednesday next, during the morning service at Lee Church. Will you and your niece come over and be present on this solemn yet joyful occasion. It will delight our hearts if you will. I know how earnestly you will both pray that the Holy Spirit would make her His own little 'living temple.'

"Again we unite in fond love and thanks to you, for consenting to be our darling's godmother. Her name is to be Lucy, which alone would give her a claim on your heart. . . . . It is the name of her mother's beloved mother, who is now in heaven, with her Saviour. . . . . Come as early as you can, and stay as late as you can. Mary and I have set our hearts on having a long day's enjoyment of you both; and you *will* love our lovely little child."

During these three years at Woolwich, Major Vandeleur devoted the larger number of the evenings in each week to conducting Bible-classes amongst the soldiers and the workmen in the Arsenal, and to taking part in various prayer-meetings. The hospital in the Arsenal was a great object of interest to him; and many of the sufferers derived comfort and blessing through his prayers and counsel, and reading of the Word of God.

One afternoon he heard that a man in the Arsenal had met with a serious accident; and as soon as his work there was over, he hastened to the hospital, to see what could be done for the comfort of the poor fellow. The doctors had just decided upon immediate amputation of his foot. The man was lamenting, not his own suffering, but the prospect of starvation before his poor wife and little children, if he were to leave the hospital a cripple for life. Arthur earnestly requested the doctors to postpone the amputation until the next day. They did not consider that the delay would involve any serious consequences, and therefore consented to it.

Arthur went home, to plead earnestly with his God on behalf of this poor man, whose distress had so moved his heart. That prayer of faith met with an immediate answer. The next morning, the doctors pronounced the foot to be so much better, that there was every reason to hope that it might be saved; and in a short time, the man entirely recovered.

But a better blessing still was given, in answer to that prayer of faith.

"The Major spoke kindly," said he, "and prayed with me, and told me about the Saviour who had bought me with His own blood. And then I began to see that I, who thought I had not a friend anywhere, had found two friends, an earthly and a Heavenly Friend. After that, I made up my mind to live a new life, by the help of God. There was room for a change, for I had never been to a school, nor to a place of worship from the time I was ten years of age. I never had a mother's prayers; and if any one spoke to me about religion, all I did was to laugh at them. As soon as I came out of hospital, I went to church, and felt very odd at first, my clothes being so shabby. But by the help of God, I got over that, and learned to love it. For the last two years I have been a teacher in a Sunday-school, and it is a blessed work."

From the time of his leaving the hospital, this man has been steadfastly walking with God; and he has been prospered in every way. His grateful love for Major Vandeleur never lessened; he rejoiced in his presence, mourned when military duty called him away; and few, amongst the many true mourners, sorrowed more sincerely over his open grave.

In the autumn of 1857, and the winter of 1857–58, Major Vandeleur took an active part in the efforts made to alleviate the distress of the families of those soldiers who had been sent off suddenly to India, when the great cry for help had reached these shores, amidst the uproar of the Indian mutiny. But no new call for exertion ever caused him to relinquish any labour of love which he had previously undertaken. Besides his week-day work for his Divine Master, he threw himself with all his heart into the superintendence and instruction of the Sunday-schools at Plumstead; and sowed seed of life there, which has since sprung up and borne much fruit.

The following letter shews in what manner he began a new year of his life :—

"Royal Arsenal, *January* 21*st*, 1858.

"I must not let the whole day pass without telling you how your kind little note has warmed, and comforted, and strengthened my heart. It is an unspeakable blessing to be remembered by those one most loves when passing the milestones of our pilgrimage towards the Celestial City.

"May God bless you for your constant kindness towards one so little worthy of being loved by any one in the world!

"You know that I do desire to be thankful,—and to shew that gratitude not only in words, but in deeds,— to Him who has done and continues to do such wonders for me and mine. I know how little I have served Him, and I do desire during this new year of my life to cleave closer to Jesus, to sit more constantly at the foot of the Cross, and to dwell under the outpouring of the Holy Ghost, and, above all things, to have a larger and more unselfish heart of love to all the world, for Christ's sake. Pray for me, and ask all that your letter contains—mercy, peace, and love; this is what I have asked, and do, and will ask for you. May you be filled with all the fulness of Christ, both now and evermore!"

In allusion to the years following his marriage, she who could best testify to his daily life, thus writes:—"In his own home, he never for one moment laid aside his religion. Indeed, only those who saw him there, could tell how heavenly was his spirit. It often struck me with a kind of awe, how intense was his longing after a state of perfect holiness; and how his spirit used to pant for the full enjoyment of his Saviour's presence."

From the same sacred memories, we have this touch-ing insight given us into his inner life:—"If anything had ruffled or annoyed him, he would take his Bible and shut himself up with it in his own room for a few minutes; and then would come forth from that lonely communing with his God and Saviour, with a counte-nance beaming with peace and love."

In the month of April, 1858, he resigned his appoint-ment of Captain-Instructor in the Arsenal, considering it to be his duty, for professional reasons, to do so. Consequent upon this resignation, he was posted to a company at Gibraltar; for which station he sailed from England on the 17th of July, to the deep regret of his many warmly-attached friends. But the emphasis of the sorrow lay with his wife and himself; as her state of health rendered it impossible for her to accompany him, in the height of summer.

The following letters were written in the months intervening between his leaving Woolwich and sailing for Gibraltar :—

TO GENERAL ANDERSON, R.A.

"LEE, April 28th, 1858.

"MY DEAREST COLONEL,—I cannot tell you how much your very kind note of sympathy and love comforted and refreshed our hearts. It found us busy packing up; so I determined to finish that work before answering it, that I might be able to write at some length. . . . .

"To look beyond second causes, I cannot but think it probable that my heavenly Father saw that my heart and thoughts were becoming of late too much engrossed with professional matters, and too little devoted to Himself. Great, eternal realities may not have been sufficiently present to my mind. It seems as if, while working for Him at the Sunday-school and at meetings of all kinds, I had not had sufficient time for meditation and prayer. 'He made me keeper of the vineyards, but mine own vineyard have I not kept.' May this be altered now! We shall, in truth, be very glad of a little quiet, especially for my precious wife's sake; for she really was overworking herself every day, and I could not prevent her.

"Every one at Woolwich is rejoiced to have Colonel and Mrs Travers back again : they are such a happy, useful, delightful pair. I was so thankful to be able to transfer into such able hands the Plumstead Sunday-school.

"The Tuesday evening readings, which we all so much enjoyed at your most hospitable house, are now held at our friend Mr Acworth's. They are still well attended, and are most harmonious and profitable.

"With our united affectionate love to Mrs Anderson and yourself, and all your family circle, believe me most affectionately and gratefully yours,

"ARTHUR VANDELEUR."

"KILTANON, *June* 1858.

"Thank you for a letter which has warmed my heart and refreshed my soul. Thank you, too, for the simple and beautiful 'revival' hymn. I doubt not that such hymns as that, have been powerful instruments in forwarding the glorious revival in America. God grant it may increase day by day! and oh that the heavenly flame may light up the darkness of this land, still so firmly held in the deadly grasp of Rome! However, I rejoice to say that the good seed is being steadily and constantly sown in the minds of the people; and our one great effort is to get them to read the Word of the living God. My Scripture-reader at Ralahine tells me that they converse freely with him, listen to all he says, are quite unable to answer his arguments, but still retain their former opinions! This makes it very up-hill work; but it is still our duty to labour on, and believe the promise that His own Word will not return unto Him void. And oh for such a gift of the Holy Spirit on all who by name are Protestants—such a fresh baptism of that Spirit upon us who do believe and trust alone in the Lord Jesus, that our lights may be burning, and the brightness may spread, and numbers around be brought from darkness to light, from the power of Satan unto God! . . . .

"This is one of the most lovely spots in Ireland; and its magnificent trees are now in all their beauty. I am regaining health and strength, thank God, every day, in this most enjoyable place; but still I should not wish to spend much time here. I miss the calls for active usefulness which were on every side at Wool-wich. A life of ease and comparative idleness, and of country pleasures, would stunt my spiritual growth.

"My darling Mary is the better for her native air. The time of our parting is drawing near, very near, now. Monday, the 21st, is the day at present fixed for it; and a bitter trial it must be to us both. But, if it lead us to seek a closer union with the Lord Jesus, and if it bring us into a fuller enjoyment of His blessed presence, and increased earnestness and use-fulness in His service—which we pray and trust that it may—then surely we ought to say, 'It is well.'"

A brother-officer of Major Vandeleur's, who was one of his most intimate friends, from the time of his joining the Royal Artillery, in looking back over the years of their acquaintance, thus wrote :—

"It was the uniform calm tenor of his whole life, his steadfast holy walk unchecked by inconsistency, that was to me the distinction of his character; *not* anything calling for special notice, or challenging observation.

"He was generous, chivalrous, and full of sympathy; tender and sensitive in his affections, more so almost than women; and, consequently, was susceptible of feeling keenly any unkindness from one he loved.

"In his opinions he was sometimes obstinate, and his temper was quick and hot. But if cause of difference arose, the slightest yielding or admission of wrong on your part was enough to disarm him instantly, and to subdue him into the gentleness of a child. He was *most* forgiving.

"His disposition was a cheerful one, and the purity and simplicity of his mind enabled him, I think, to taste pleasure with a freshness that perhaps natures less chaste seldom know. There was a frankness and sincerity about him, combined with a courtesy truly winning and attractive.

"But above these qualities, for which he might well

be loved, there dwelt within him a spirit of deep and ardent love to God, and attachment to His service. He devoted himself, and all that was his, I believe, to his Lord and Master with fervent, supreme affection. All he said and did with reference to things sacred, was marked by a reverence and awe so rare as to be most impressive. This was such a deep and settled condition of his inner life, visible in every tone and gesture, as to be the most striking feature of his character.

"To him prayer and the study of God's Word were, I believe, the atmosphere of his spiritual life, and its necessary food."

———

We saw him as he passed through London on his way to Gibraltar. A shadow had fallen upon that bright brow, and the joyous smile and manner were chastened. Something like a presentiment came over our hearts that he was going through his last and ripening trial.

CHAPTER XIV.

The Shadow of Death.

"What is it, Lord?   Dost Thou intend
  That patience should take root in me?
  Is it Thy will my will to bend,
  That I more like a child may be?

"Is it to raise my heart above
  All earthly joy and earthly pleasure,
  And loose my hands from earthly love,
  To fill them full of heavenly treasure?

"To hinder this poor mortal clinging,
  And set my heart from earth-bonds free!
  O God, my spirit art Thou bringing
  Nearer to leaving all for Thee?

"Whatever be Thy gracious thought,
  Let me not lose its sweet design;
  Since Jesus hath the blessing bought,
  Oh, for His sake, may it be mine!"

MAJOR VANDELEUR arrived in Gibraltar, at an unhealthy season of the year. His letters from that station were written in a tone of depression unusual for him, which was sufficiently to be accounted for by the separation it involved from those he loved best on earth.

Yet beyond this, like a distant knell, there fell upon our hearts a dull sense of undefined dread, as again and again, in his letters, we traced that the subject of death was frequently recurring to his mind. The following extract is but one amongst many of this nature :—

"GIBRALTAR, November 11th, 1858.

"Thank you again and again for your letter, so full of the truest sympathy and comfort. How I wish you could see my beautiful book-stand, filled with all my favourite books! I have just added to them 'The Story of Thomas Ward,' which has returned to me from a round of visits. The evening it arrived, I read it aloud to a dear young friend and fellow-disciple of the Lord Jesus. How striking is the description of the awful struggle which Satan makes to secure his prey, when he feels it eluding his grasp! This is a subject which has occupied my thoughts much of late. David could say in anticipation, 'Though I walk through the valley of the shadow of death, I will fear no evil, for Thou art with me;' but when we are actually entering the dark valley, and we feel life ebbing fast, then must it be much more difficult to say, 'I fear no evil.' But, as God taught you to shew poor Ward, and as Ryle points out in that powerful tract, 'Never Perish,' *then*, as at all times, what we must do is to take our great God and Saviour simply at His word—'No man is able to pluck them out of my Father's hand;' 'Neither shall any pluck them out of my hand.' Oh for grace and strength to rest upon these precious, blessed truths when the solemn hour of death shall come! . . . . You will rejoice to know that God has enabled me to do a little work for Him since I have been out here. Indeed, I now see many good reasons why He has sent me out, and I know that they are all full of mercy. Thank you dearly for writing to my darling wife. As far as I can see my way at present, it is best that she should not come out to me, as I hope to return by the end of February. But it is a sore trial, especially in such a place as this, the monotony of which is almost overwhelming. I work almost daily at my photography, and have lately been very successful. It is a good thing to have such a source of recreation. . . . .

"There is a great spirit of religious inquiry alive amongst our officers ; and I have had some interesting and hopeful conversation with several of them; but the great difficulty with some is to take the next step— the all-important one of deciding for God. Some of us meet every Tuesday evening, for reading the Scripture and prayer, and I hope not without spiritual improvement.

" Dearest Mr Chalmers wrote to me so affectionately some time since ; and your beloved sister added some of her kind, sweet words, which I greatly prized. Mr Chalmers' letter was a real blessing to me. I have been hoping to hear again from one of the beloved family.

" With earnest blessings, and affectionate love, your ever grateful and loving

"ARTHUR VANDELEUR."

EXTRACTS FROM LETTERS TO HIS WIFE.

"SOUTHAMPTON, *July 17th*, 1858.

" My heart is growing deeply sad at the prospect of going so very far away from you, my most beloved one, and from my sweet little child. My work being all over now, I have more time to think, and more time to pray for you and her. Indeed, though sad, I am far from being without much to comfort me. I cannot tell you how the excessive kindness of all our friends has overwhelmed me. What a blessed, holy thing is Christian love and friendship! Oh for a grateful heart to Him who has bestowed such wondrous and constant proofs of His love upon me, the most unworthy of His servants!"

"*October 13th.*

"Blessed be God for continued good tidings of you, and of the darling babe, and our sweet little Lucy. . . . . You will, I know, rejoice with me that another officer has joined our little Tuesday readings. We have had four meetings, and as none of us are very learned, we bring all kinds of books and commentaries to bear on our subject. We have just finished the seven churches in Revelations. I think we all enjoy them, and I am sure they are profitable to our souls. I think I am gradually finding out why God has sent me here. I trust He is making me of some use amongst the young officers. Pray earnestly for me, that I may be enabled to lead some of them steadily to Jesus, and pray that my example may be of as much use as anything I may say to them. Oh for a consistent and holy walk and conversation!"

"*November 25th.*

"You will be glad to hear I have at length roused my coward heart to visit the hospital, and speak to the poor men who are on the brink of eternity. I think some of them were pleased with my visit. Yesterday I took them our dearest friend's cards of prayer, and read aloud in one of the rooms her letter to the navvies. May it please God to bless these feeble efforts to the making known the glorious gospel of Jesus Christ among our soldiers! The hospital-sergeant—-Sergeant Batson—is a truly good man ; and one of the orderlies, named Cole, is also a devoted Christian. Our little Tuesday meetings have gone on regularly. I think they are a blessing to us all. All but myself are young Christians, and it is delightful to see the earnestness of their first love."

" Nearly Midnight, December 31st.

" The remembrance of the wonderful goodness of our God to us of old time is still present to my mind, and it makes me fully trust His infinite love. Still, the continuance of this painful separation, and the uncertainty of our time of meeting again, out of which I can see no way, is a great trial.

" January 1st.

" It has now struck twelve, and I have just risen from my knees, after earnestly seeking forgiveness for all my sins that are past, from Him who has promised that He will, for Jesus Christ's sake, blot out as a cloud our transgressions, and as a thick cloud our sins. I have asked that, during the year now opening, we may both be strengthened with His glorious might in our souls, and enabled to serve and glorify Him more than we ever yet have done.

"For my precious wife and children I have asked, from the bountiful Giver of all good, multitudes of the richest blessings. It went straight to my heart, a little while ago, to read, in 'Nelson on Infidelity,' the following note :—'They believe that the Man of Calvary can do whatever He pleases, and that, if any love Him, He frequently does please that they shall have almost anything for which they ask. None but His *obedient children*, however, know this fact by *experience.*' That you may know it now and ever *experimentally*, my beloved wife, is my constant and earnest prayer."

"*January 21st.*

"My birth-day. I believe you have remembered it, and are thinking of me. For thirty long years has my life been spared; and, oh, how few of them have been heartily spent in His service who died to redeem me, and how multiplied have been my transgressions against all His love! I have been cast down to-day by the remembrance of my guilt; but my hope is truly in His never-failing mercy; and He has, and does comfort me with all the precious promises in the 31st and 32nd Psalms. May our blessed Lord and Master so strengthen me with the promised aid of His Holy Spirit as to enable me, for the short remainder of my stay here, constantly, and with self-denial, to serve and glorify Him, whose service is joy and peace, and whose gift—not wages—is eternal life through Jesus Christ our Lord !

" Grace, mercy, and peace be multiplied unto thee, my own precious wife, now, and through life; and through life to our sweet little children, too.—Ever your own loving husband."

" *February* 11*th*.

" This prolonged separation, my own darling wife, is indeed a severe trial. I feel it has been ordered for us, to prevent our thinking too much of each other, and to cause Him, whom we should love infinitely more than any earthly being, to become dearer and more precious to our souls. I often wonder whether it has really had this effect upon my stubborn, selfish, indolent heart; but I do not know that I can say so. I long, and try oftentimes, to realise truly the invisible presence of my Saviour God; but all seems in vain. If I could feel Him close to me every hour of the day, how different would my life be from what it now is! but I almost think that if it were so, my joy and peace would be almost more than this poor body could endure. In His own good time, this corruptible shall put on incorruption, and this mortal shall put on immortality, and then shall I see Him as He is—all beauty, light, holiness, and love."

"February 18th.

"My beloved wife, you must not long or pray too much for my return to you. Our first, most constant, most earnest wishes and prayers, must be for a growing likeness to Jesus, a more intense sense of dutifulness, and more true Christian humility. All things beside must be far below these in our hearts, if we would walk so as to please Him; and not require the check of His correcting hand. . . . . It is Sunday morning now. May it be a holy, blessed, soul-refreshing day to my own wife; and may the infinite love of the Triune Jehovah rest upon her and upon our darlings, for all eternity!"

"March 3rd.

"My heart bounds for joy as I read the sweet over-flowings of yours, on the most momentous of all subjects. Indeed, it will be delightful when we can again kneel together before the Throne of Grace, and pour out our souls in praise and prayer.

"The Maberlys have been kindness itself to me, ever since they arrived. I dine with them, on an average, twice a-week, and like them so very much. They have three dear little children, who are great chums of mine.

"I am now safely ensconced in my new house. How glad I am that I may have but a few short weeks to spend in it! Hope tells me I have really some chance of going home in April, and this is March. I trust I am not too anxious about it; indeed I desire to be patient, and to submit to the infinitely wise arrangements of Him who so truly loves us; but the longing desire to be with you and my beloved children, is almost irrepressible occasionally. I feel our lives may not be long spared; indeed I often fancy mine is held by a more than usually precarious tenure, and this makes my heart yearn the more for the enjoyment, while I may be spared, of the society of those who are so unspeakably precious to me.

"Oh for grace truthfully to say, 'Nevertheless, not what I will, but what Thou wilt!'"

Notwithstanding this burden on his spirits, and these deep yearnings to spend all that was left of life to him, with those whom he so fondly loved; yet, without one exception, all who associated with him bear testimony to the serene cheerfulness of his daily companionship, and to his earnest delight in the work of His heavenly Master. A young officer who was speaking of him to me some months ago, said — "Everybody on the Old Rock liked Vandeleur, and regretted him when he left us. He was 'blue'* you know; but then he was *such a bright* blue! No gay man, I should think, was ever half so truly cheerful and charming as a companion."

And a young friend of my own, who was also

* A slang term for being religious.

quartered with him at Gibraltar,* bears a similar testimony, with still more earnest personal affection :—
"Major Vandeleur was always consistent and cheerful; and was wonderfully liked and looked up to by all who knew him. I shall ever remember his joyous smile when he read to me some text which had reference to our subject of conversation, or which he particularly loved, or found comfort from, in the trial of separation from his wife and children."

Captain Warden, C.B., of the Royal Navy, who commands the harbour at Gibraltar, thus writes of Major Vandeleur (by whom his friendship had been greatly valued) :—

"He was in the habit of attending a weekly meeting at Mr Crozier's, for prayer and Scripture-reading; and he was accompanied by several young officers of the corps, who were first led thither, I believe, by his influence and by his example.

"He was one of the few men to be met with in the world, in whose company it was impossible to be, without discovering that his heart and life were devoted to that Master and Saviour, of whom he was so distinguished a servant.

"For myself, I can truly say, that I never took to any one more readily, or with more hearty admiration."

With Captain Jackson, R.A., Arthur had also formed a true friendship.

* Lieutenant Hamilton, R.A.

"He knew when he was here," writes Captain Jackson, from Gibraltar, "that he was not to be long for this world; and he used to talk to me about it.

"Five or six years ago, I met him for the first time in a railway carriage between Woolwich and Blackheath. We were perfect strangers, but in the course of conversation he remarked, 'How happy it was to *know* that one had a Saviour!'

"I have always remembered his saying that; it led me often to think and wonder how it could be. . . . . And now I have reason, indeed, to be very thankful to him for the many happy and profitable hours which I spent in his company here."

A faithful servant who was with Arthur at Gibraltar, remembers hearing one of the hospital-sergeants remark, that, "of all who visited the sick men, Major Vandeleur seemed to feel the most *hurt* at their sufferings."

This servant also recollects that he was in the habit of speaking earnestly to the men in the batteries, both about their duty as soldiers and about the happiness offered them, through believing in the Saviour of the world.

There was one man who was continually getting into disgrace, from drinking and other snares. The week before Major Vandeleur left Gibraltar, he spoke words of kind advice and sympathy to this poor man, who was then undergoing punishment. From that day forth, the soldier transgressed no more. It was his *last* disgrace. He said to Major Vandeleur's servant, "Those kind words did more for me than all the punishments in the world."

From the same person, we learn that Major Vandeleur seemed never to be weary of well-doing. When his failing health obliged him now and then to stop for an hour, to recruit his exhausted strength, he would rise up afterwards with fresh ardour to return to his blessed work. And when military duty called him up early, or kept him up late, he never allowed himself to shorten the time which he had set apart for reading the Bible and for prayer.

The following sketch of his life at Gibraltar is written by Sergeant-Major Garnham :—

"Major Vandeleur joined the brigade of Royal Artillery at Gibraltar during the month of July, 1858. His appearance, though delicate, was not such as to cause any immediate apprehension.

"The weather at that season is very sultry, and the place not unfrequently enveloped by Levanters, a heavy mist caused by an east wind from the Mediterranean, which is very injurious not only to the health of new-comers, but even of 'Old Rockers.' It is known by the name of 'Kill-Johnny.' In fact, almost the whole of the summer season is unfavourable to persons in delicate health.

"Major Vandeleur, however, at once assumed, and performed with his accustomed cheerfulness, those various and arduous duties which devolve upon an artillery officer in a large fortress. Not long before this, an order had been issued from the Horse Guards, directing that the armaments of the more conspicuous batteries should be replaced by guns of a heavier calibre. This remodelling was afterwards carried out so extensively, that scarcely a battery remained unaffected by its provision. It will be easily understood that, at such a crisis, the duties and responsibilities of the artillery officer were much increased, and that it required the greatest vigilance on the part of those under whose immediate superintendence this re-organization was carried out, to avoid the occurrence of serious accidents.

"Firm in maintaining his command, gentle in its exercise, laborious in his regimental duties, affable and courteous to all, the influence of his graceful kindliness was widely felt. Rich veins of anecdote, interesting in style and eminently Christian in tone, distinguished his address. Many of the men to whom, without disdain of their humbler rank, he would often address himself, remember them well, and the beautiful manner in which they were told.

"Chiefly must his brother officers have felt the

holy influence that breathed around him.   His example told most powerfully.   Many of them resolved to 'go with him,' convinced 'that he would do them good.'   They were not disappointed.   God acknowledged his intercessions, and blessed his efforts, and they—his sons or brothers in Christ Jesus—joined him in his holy enterprise for the recovery of ruined souls.

"On Sunday mornings, in the regimental school, and from day to day throughout the week, in one place or another, they were to be seen meeting him, to receive his counsel as to their work, and his loving encouragement concerning it.   Several ladies, too, joined him in earnest efforts for the spiritual good of the children of the Sunday-school.   They were of all religious denominations; they numbered generally about eighty, girls and boys; their ages ranged from about four to twelve years.   As it was conducted on liberal principles, when the classes were dismissed the pupils were allowed to go to their several places of worship.   Major Vandeleur was greatly beloved by the children; especially by those in his own class.   This was owing to the kind and affectionate manner with which he taught them, and his happy mode of management.   And he was reverenced as much as he was loved.

"Each child had a portion of Scripture to commit to memory, and to repeat.   The Major would then catechise them upon what they had learnt.   A chapter in the Bible was next read and explained,—questions being asked from time to time. Should their attention slacken, he would tell some short, striking Christian anecdote, at which their faces used to brighten up, while they listened with an eager and delighted attention. As a further encouragement, he purchased reference Bibles for his class, teaching them their use. He also lent them books and periodicals to read at home, and would occasionally mark his sense of their good behaviour by inviting one of their number to his quarters. This indeed was a treat not to be forgotten. He was always most liberal in everything that tended to the advancement and the amusement of the children; and his abrupt departure, with its sorrowful explanation, was long and deeply regretted by them all. He very kindly left as a memento in the school, a beautiful concertina, which had been previously lent by him to accompany the children in their singing.

"As an officer, he took the deepest interest in the temporal and spiritual welfare of the men under his command; and, as a natural result, was much beloved and respected by them.

"He was most successful, whilst detached with his battery at Europa Point, in assembling, in conjunction with the chaplain, evening classes for the purpose of reading and explaining the Scriptures, as well as in giving short Bible lectures, at once most interesting and impressive. The men would frequently express in earnest terms their gratitude for what they had heard, and for the kindly manner in which they had been addressed.

"On wet Sundays, it is the custom in Gibraltar, to have prayers read by the officers in the several barracks. I well remember a sergeant telling me after one of these services, 'that the lieutenant on duty had read prayers, and that the Major had given them a sort of sermon in a most feeling and striking manner, and that he should never forget his earnestness.' He said he had never seen the men more riveted.

"The Major was most assiduous in encouraging men who were anxious to read and improve themselves, by lending them books.

"He was a regular visitor at the hospital, and always shewed deep interest in the temporal and spiritual welfare of the patients, and particularly directed his attention to those who were seriously afflicted. Often would he fervently pray by the bedside of the sick and suffering soldier, after reading a suitable portion of Scripture. He would also leave behind a goodly supply of religious tracts and periodicals. 'God bless you all!' came so warm from his heart, on leaving the various wards, that they were cold hearts indeed which did not respond to its affectionate fervour."

Month after month of Arthur's sojourn at Gibraltar had been passed in awaiting the anticipated recall of his company, at this time rendered probable by changes which were being made in the organisation of the Artillery, and by the augmentation of the Regiment. But, towards April, increasing illness made it plain that duty no longer claimed him at Gibraltar. The regimental surgeons ordered him home for three months; and, immediately on his arrival in London, the Medical Board, before which he appeared, ratified the order, with an addition of five months more.

CHAPTER XV

Near Home.

"My Jesus, as Thou wilt!
   Oh, may Thy will be mine!
Into Thy hand of love
   I would my all resign.

"Through sorrow, or through joy,
   Conduct me as Thine own,
And help me still to say,
   My Lord, Thy will be done!

"Straight to my home above
   I travel calmly on,
And sing, in life or death,
   My Lord, Thy will be done!"

WITH failing health. but with a glad and thankful heart, Arthur Vandeleur hastened to Ireland, to rejoin his wife and children.

The first letter which he wrote to me, after that blessed meeting, is an overflow of a heart, in the full tide of grateful adoration to a prayer-hearing God. He said nothing about his own state of health.

It was from Mrs Vandeleur that we learned the unfavourable opinion of his case, which was entertained by his medical advisers ; and still the darkest side of it was partially concealed from her. On him, it made but a passing impression. That hopefulness of disposition which was his characteristic, had sprung up with regard to his recovery, the moment he felt a little better, and was restored to his wife and babes.

The first few happy weeks, after their long separation, were passed in the lovely scenery of Killarney. In the midst of this time of deep and tranquil enjoyment, some business which required immediate attention, obliged Major Vandeleur to be in London for a few hours.　Allusion to that flying visit is made in the following letter :—

"RAILWAY HOTEL, KILLARNEY, *May 24th*, 1859.

"It almost made up for my great disappointment at missing you, both at Beckenham and in London, on Wednesday, to receive such a dear letter of hearty regret.　Blessings on you for it!　But still I should so have enjoyed even á few minutes' meeting.　What a charming tea-party and meeting dear Anstruther had for the members of the Guards' Bible-classes, at Wellington Barracks!　It did my heart good to listen to all that he and dear Mr Chalmers and Captain Trotter said.　It seemed to me that God was present there, giving a time of refreshing and blessing, both to those who spoke and those who listened.

"Oh, what a happiness to be at home, amongst be-loved friends again!　Goodness and mercy are indeed following me all my days, and by and by I shall dwell in the house of the Lord for ever.　And not alone, but with all those whom I love so much in Jesus.　Glory be to the grace of our God!"

"KILTANON, *July 15th*, 1859.

"We have had a most delightful time in this much-loved home of my darling wife.　Dearest Hattie's marriage was a very cheerful one ; and she has a bright prospect of happiness before her.　God bless her and

her husband, and realise it to them both, to the uttermost !

"A large number of relatives were congregated for
the marriage, and they helped to cheer her dear father,
for whom we were dreading the departure of his last
daughter, from daily life under his roof.

"Their aunts from Leamington were here. Such
dear people ! 'Aunt Agnes' is always on the look-
out to do kind and unselfish things. I believe it is
from the motive, which I long to have in fuller force
in my own heart—grateful love of the Lord Jesus
Christ. Constantly do I wish and pray that this love
may be my all in all, the centre and fountain of all
other love ; and the ruling, guiding, consecrating
power of every feeling or my neart.

"It is so difficult to regard every one around you in
the light that God sees them—as immortal souls
who must live or die eternally. What I desire is, to
be made so Christ-like as to love, for their souls' sake,
those whose natural characters do not attract me.
Souls, 'for whom Christ died,' whom the Father
loved so well as to spare His only Son that He might
redeem them by His blood, and in whom the Holy
Ghost is willing to come and dwell—should have points
enough of interest for us !

"It was so kind of you to write whilst you are enjoying a few days at pleasant Terling. Darling Mary
and I would greatly like to pay another visit to the

dear friends there. How nice it would be if you could meet us, as in those few days when they so kindly allowed me to join that family-gathering, soon after my return from the Crimea.

"What glorious news is this of the Revival in the north of Ireland! There is too much of the stamp of heaven about its blessed results to leave any doubt that the work is of God.

"I quite agree with you that one would be thankful, if there were none of those distressing outward symptoms. But try to prevent our friends in England from disbelieving the reality of the work, because of this accompaniment. They should remember the excitability of the national character; and especially that, wherever there is a work of God, Satan will try to do all the damage to it that he can.

"Will you ask our friends to pray that the Revival may spread towards the south-west of Ireland? I have great hopes that it may. About four thousand persons have been attending open-air preaching in Limerick. Ah, if the warm Irish hearts should receive 'the truth as it is in Jesus,' nothing more would be wanted to make the country that which Dan O'Connell so often boasted—

> ' First flower of the earth,
> And first gem of the sea!'

"God be praised for the welcome news of peace! We can hardly expect it to be of long continuance; but any respite from the dire calamity of war is a blessing indeed."

During this visit to Ireland, having occasion to meet his tenantry with reference to an election, he assembled them afterwards by his mother's grave ; and there, in words which touched every heart, besought them to follow her, and to come with him, to Jesus Christ and glory.

For a time after his return to Woolwich, our hearts were cheered by his evident power of rallying. There seemed too much life and energy about him to be associated with the idea of a hopeless malady. He believed himself to be recovering, and rejoiced in the thought of prolonged life devoted to his Saviour's service.

"OSMASTON MANOR, *September 24th*, 1859.

"We are thoroughly enjoying our little holiday. It is most refreshing to us to be in the midst of a family so entirely given to the Lord, and to His work ; and, most of all, to enjoy communion and fellowship with that most dear fellow and devoted Christian, Stevenson Blackwood, and his truly noble wife. We have had some delightful meetings for reading the Bible, conversation, and prayer, suggested by him ; and both darling Mary and I have felt it 'good for us to be there.' You will, I know, pray for us, that all we have seen and heard here may rouse us up to a more thorough devotion of body, soul, and spirit, to our blessed Master's cause, the winning souls of every age and rank and race to serve in the great army of Jesus Christ the Lord. I hope and pray that it may be so, and I think it will, and, oh, how full of joy and unalloyed delight that blessed service is! No tongue can tell but they who have been permitted to enlist under the blessed banner of the great Captain of our salvation."

" MARYON ROAD, WOOLWICH,
December 3rd, 1859.

"It has been a great sorrow to me not to be able for so many days to answer your very precious letter. Duty of all kinds, not to be avoided or neglected, must plead my excuse. I have been worked to the utmost of my strength, but, thank God, not beyond it. How shall we thank you enough, for all your prayers for us. Surely they have been heard, for in every way, both in spiritual and temporal things, the hand of the Lord has been over us for good. Oh for hearts filled to the brim with gratitude and love! Since our delightful visit to you, we have been to Birch Hall, and enjoyed our stay there, thoroughly. We came in for the Annual Bible Society Meeting at Colchester, which we liked so much. We returned to our home, greatly refreshed, both in soul and body.

"The work here is going on very nicely and steadily.

Our adult gunner classes on Friday evenings give us all much pleasure and encouragement. I have given to many of mine those dear little red books; and last night they told me so earnestly that they liked them very much indeed. I do believe that God is touching the hearts of many by the mighty power of His Holy Spirit. Glory and praise be unto Him, to all eternity!

"Our best love to all beneath that blessed Rectory roof."

A staff-sergeant of the Royal Artillery who met Major Vandeleur one evening in a street of the town of Woolwich; remembers that after conversing with him earnestly, and encouraging him to persevere in seeking to follow that Saviour whom he had already chosen to serve, Major Vandeleur told him how much interest and sympathy he felt with those sergeants who had been selected to visit their sick comrades in the hospital; and then alluding to a book called the "Sunday-school Teacher's Treasury," from which he had derived great help in imparting instruction, he said he thought it would be a valuable aid to them in their labours of love. Finding that the non-commissioned officers did not possess it, he gave the sergeant a sovereign for the purchase of four copies, one for himself, one to be deposited in the Soldiers' Institute, and two to be given to the other sergeants appointed to read in the hospital. Then, shaking hands with him, he bade him "Look to Jesus, the author and finisher of his faith."

"This commendation to a Saviour's love and grace," writes the sergeant,* who has requested that this anecdote be recorded, "appears as if it were repeated to me, in those kind, earnest tones, every time I revisit the grave where lie the loved remains of Major Vandeleur."

"28 Maryon Road, Woolwich,
December 22nd, 1859.

"My dear General,—Among the many blessings it has been my privilege to enjoy since my return to Woolwich in August last, not one has awakened a deeper thrill of gratitude and thankfulness than the arrival of your most kind, affectionate, and welcome letter. We most heartily thank God for it, and for all it contains. It is delightful to know that you and dearest Mrs Anderson continue to remember us in any way, but especially in prayer. Who can tell how many of our multitude of blessings we owe to those prayers of yours, our dear and very valued friends!

"There is much going on about us that I know will interest you; and as you ask me to be minute, I must try to obey, like a good soldier.

"I will first speak of Woolwich generally. In spiritual matters you will rejoice to know that there is a great extension of the Lord's work going on

* Sergeant-Major Revill.

around us. You were permitted to sow much seed, and I trust, please God, that you may live to see and know that it is bearing much fruit unto life eternal. There is as yet nothing that should be called a revival in Woolwich, generally, but there are evident signs that the reviving shower is gradually coming over us, and we are beginning to feel the first drops of the longed-for blessing. The Plumstead Sunday-schools, and those in the Arsenal—the former under that devoted man Travers, the latter under dear Orr—are giving evident token that the Holy Spirit is working in an unwonted and special manner. Colonel Travers assures me that the whole tone of the schools is changed, and that many of the children are evidently converted ; and so much heartfelt interest and earnestness is manifested, that it only remains for him to guide and regulate its expression, and to direct it into the proper channel.

"Mr Hare has obtained the consent of the Commandant—who, I rejoice to say, favours everything which would tend to promote the best welfare of the soldier—to allow any of the men who might feel so inclined, to devote an hour of their school-time on Friday evenings, to religious instruction. Classes have been formed, and many volunteers come to them ; and we have thus a better chance than we ever had before for getting at the hearts of the full-grown soldiers. We have about seven classes, and an average attendance of about one hundred ; and it is delightful to observe the sober and even anxious earnestness, with which these men listen to the gospel call. Oh that He who has thus opened a wide door, may of His mercy bring many lost sheep back into the only true Fold—Jesus Christ!

"Mr Hare is now the rallying-point for the officers of the garrison. I never go to his house on Tuesday evenings without thinking of the happy meetings we have so often enjoyed in your well-remembered house on the common. The meetings are very well attended, as many as thirty-five sometimes being present.

"You most kindly ask after ourselves. I had, at last, to come home from Gibraltar on sick leave. My lungs were much affected, but, thank God, only with chronic bronchitis; and since my return, I have rapidly and steadily gained health and strength, although I feel this severe weather. It is delightful to have sufficient strength to work for our blessed Lord and Master; and this we try to do every day. Our little ones are both flourishing, and are growing most attractive; indeed, my very dear friend, we are surrounded with blessings, and have every moment fresh occasions for praise.

"Ever your very grateful and affectionate friend,

"ARTHUR VANDELEUR."

On Friday, in the second week of January 1860— that week which encircled the globe with an atmosphere of prayer, the warmth and light of which, by the grace of God, have not yet faded away—a special prayer-meeting for the army was held at the Barn at Beckenham.

Arthur Vandeleur came over to us for that meeting; and then, for the first time, we began to realise that he was in a hopeless decline. Seldom, if ever, have I seen a spirit so brave and strong, in a frame so weakened and attenuated. He was as cheerful as ever; but it was a most hallowed cheerfulness, like that of one who kept the eternal realities ever before him.

A dear young friend was with us that night, to whom, when he was entering on his course of military education at Addiscombe College, Arthur Vandeleur had spoken words of wise and loving counsel, which had been greatly blessed to his stablishing and strengthening in the Christian life. To learn that those brief words had been thus owned of God, was one of the many good gifts, of a similar nature, which seemed to have been kept, through the tender love of the Divine Master, to cheer His faithful servant during the last suffering months of his life.

Ill as he was, he still insisted upon accompanying us to the meeting; and there he poured out his soul in prayer for the army, with a holy fervour which few who heard him could forget.

A solemn and sorrowful impression was left upon our hearts that night. Passing, as it did, like a common evening, and mingled, though he was, in all our interests, we still silently felt that he stood apart from us, as the dying from the living, and that in the place where that beloved voice had so often been lifted up in prayer, it would be heard no more for ever.

"MARYON ROAD, *January* 21*st*, 1860.

"I cannot dream of allowing this happy day to close, without sending some answer, however unworthy, to that loved letter, so full of precious prayer and birth-day blessings, which greeted me this morning. . . . .

"I trust you will have such a blessed day with Mr Radcliffe, as we had last Sunday, in the Scottish church. It was deeply solemn and awakening. His appeal to the unconverted was very powerful. The impression on my mind the whole time was, that, as of old, 'the power of the Lord was present to heal.' . . . . How earnestly we should pray for one who has been so owned of God, that he may be kept humble and holy, and have a right judgment given him in all things. . . . . Could you come and stay with us for a few days, it would be better than pounds of tonics and quinine to my Mary and me. If it might seem good to my God, I would desire of Him rather more health and strength than I possess at present. But He knows what is most for His glory and my good; and on this day I especially desire to commit myself, body and soul, to His blessed keeping. Thus, and thus only, ALL IS WELL."

Up to the middle of February, notwithstanding his gradually increasing weakness and illness, he still scrupulously performed all his duties as a field-officer; and almost every leisure evening which he had, was devoted to attending the prayer-meetings at Woolwich, or to holding a Bible-class of soldiers. His gunners' class was a source of the deepest interest to him. He loved the men, and was repaid by their warm and reverent affection, and far *more* than rewarded by the good hope that many of them were led to seek and find salvation through Jesus Christ.

On the 10th of February, he attended the annual meeting at Woolwich, for the Soldiers' Scripture Society. It was his last public effort of the kind. Some who heard him compared his speech to a silver cord, which drew the hearts of all the hearers to himself, and with him, up to the very gate of heaven.

After this, he was for some time confined to his house by an attack of fever and ague. But his sympathies were as fresh as ever, as will be seen by the letter which follows :—

"WOOLWICH, *Saturday Evening.*

"Your welcome letter of sympathy and love has been a cordial to my heart ever since it came. We prayed most earnestly for you, that your visits to the ships at ——, might be productive of great results, in bringing many souls to Jesus by the power of His

Spirit. May He cause His own work to spread on all sides !

" I have heard to-day that a few of the cadets, at Woolwich, are making a stand on the Lord's side. Will not this rejoice the heart of our dear friend, Major Gibb? How charming it will be if a little band should unite together here in prayer and in reading the Bible, like those dear young Christians at Addiscombe ! I have already been requested to lend a helping hand to one 'who earnestly desires to be kept from falling into sin.' That is a call to be attended to, *at once*.

" Your dear Bob was down at Woolwich last week. It did my heart good to look upon his face again ; and to hear his pleasant cheery talk, with his clear, bright thoughts upon subjects of highest interest. I love him dearly.

" There are some very earnest Christians now, thank God, amongst my brother-officers here ; and the work of the Lord is prospering in their hands. If you will come and spend a day with us soon, we shall have a great deal to tell you which will cheer your heart, and make you bless and praise our God and Father in Christ Jesus."

In the month of March, Major and Mrs Vandeleur spent a few days at Hastings, and the sea-breezes seemed for the time to rally his failing powers. He returned to Woolwich to find that, through the influence of his friend Colonel Tulloh, he had been appointed Assistant-Inspector of Artillery. It was with peculiar pleasure that he found himself again employed in the Arsenal : the appointment was especially suited to his tastes and talents, and the prospect of holding it under Colonel Tulloh, who had treated him with unvarying kindness, and whose friendship he had long valued, gave an additional zest to his gratification in the matter. But deeply touching was it, to all who watched his declining health, to witness the efforts he made to battle with rapidly-increasing disease, and to fulfil his duties to the uttermost. Each day his kind and considerate " chief " urged him to take more rest; but almost every morning found him at his post, with unabated spirit and energy, determined to go through the work of the day, although returning home each afternoon, completely exhausted in mind and body; for he had now reached that advanced stage of consumption, which deprives most of its victims of the power of even rising from their beds.

No one could be a visitor under his roof, at this time, without marvelling at the exceeding grace of God that was in him. His warmth of temper—which was not without its charm for those who loved him, because they knew so well that one gentle word was enough, at any moment, to melt him into generous tenderness and touching acknowledgment of error—was now kept under the most watchful control.

There had always been a remarkable contrast between his almost morbid sensitiveness to the slightest ridicule, touching himself or his friends, and his holy boldness and utter disregard of the sneer of the world when directed against his fearless religion, and the open honour which he set upon all things belonging to his King, and for His sake, upon all those whom he believed to be serving Him. But now, the love of that Redeemer seemed to flow as the river of God, which is full of water, through the channel of that human soul. Every concern of His kingdom to the remotest end of the earth, had an interest and a charm for him. And his "love of the brethren," seemed to give one a glimpse into the world of love beyond the veil, which was already almost transparent to his eyes.

On the 12th of April, he wrote—" I am now, blessed be the holy name of my Lord and Master, much better as to the attack of fever and ague, although very weak still. During my long illness, many indeed have been the striking and most beautiful tokens of my precious Saviour's love; and at times I have been able to rejoice in Him with all my heart and soul. At other times, my mind seems to have partaken of the feebleness of my body, and I could hardly even bear to *think*. It has been a long trial for my Mary; but she bears up most nobly, and never seems to remember herself. It is a great comfort to have her brothers, dear Trevor and Charles, here; they are so full of affectionate kindness and sympathy.

"I am writing from my birthday inkstand—my drum with arms piled. How lovely it is! I believe it was cut out of a nugget!! And the rifles are perfect. It stands always on the little table by my side; and it seems to speak to me of one who has (now, for years past,) with a mother's watchful tenderness, cared for my welfare and happiness and comfort. Blessings on her, exceeding abundantly above all that I can ask or think!

"I have two books to send as Easter gifts for dear Kennie and little Dalzell, when your beloved sister drives over again. How refreshing is all intercourse with her sweet and loving spirit!"

Thus, to the last, was all that could give pleasure, by word or deed, to friend or child, ever thoughtfully remembered by him.

TO GENERAL ANDERSON, R.A.

"28 Maryon Road, Charlton,
April 17*th*, 1860.

"My dear General,—Your most kind letter of sympathy and congratulation on my recent appointment to the Arsenal, was a true cordial to my own and my precious wife's heart.

"Truly, such a letter is more to be prized than a bag of gold placed in the hand.

"Since I last wrote, we have been at Hastings on

leave, for the sake of the mild, pure air, as I have been seriously ill, the last three months; but I am now, through God's mercy, nearly well again, though very weak. My beloved wife also is far from strong; but it is most cheering to see her untiring energy in the work of the Lord.

"Shortly before the *Himalaya* started for China, with troops, our excellent friend Mrs Thompson had prayed and read the Scriptures with one or two sergeants, and they promised to try to get together a Scripture-reading class on board. They did so; and one of them wrote from Alexandria to Mrs Thompson, to tell her that eleven non-commissioned officers and several men had joined the class. What noble influence these pious men may exert in China, among both English and Chinese! May they be given grace and strength to 'endure hardness as good soldiers of Jesus Christ!'

"Travers continues to speak with deep thankfulness of the work of God's Holy Spirit in the Plumstead School; so many lads and girls are decidedly converted to God. In Orr's school, in the Arsenal, there is also a great deal to delight and encourage.—Ever yours most affectionately,

"A. VANDELEUR."

In the month of May, whilst Major and Mrs Vandeleur were spending a few days in London with their sympathising and beloved friends, Mr and Mrs Round, the medical advisers whom he then consulted, urged upon him the duty of at once resigning his appointment in the Arsenal.

"After taking a short time for prayer on the subject," wrote Mrs Vandeleur, "my beloved husband resigned his will with the most lovely and cheerful submission to the will of his Father in heaven. For some weeks past he had felt that, should he be called to make this sacrifice, it would be a terrible trial, and he had feared that he would not be able to bear it patiently. But when the trial came, the needed grace came with it; and beautiful it was to see the smile which lighted up his face, as he said, 'Then, my Mary, it must be given up—Yes! and without one murmur.'"

In the course of the following day I received this letter from him. It proved to be the last which he ever wrote me:—

"5 SUSSEX SQUARE, LONDON,
May 15th, 1860.

"You shall be the very first to receive a letter from me, in our deep trouble. Our heavenly Father sustains us both; but it is a terrible blow. Dr Watson has this morning declared me quite unfit for work at present, and could not even give me any hope of being ready for it soon.

"You know what all this involves; the giving up of the appointment so pleasant to work in, and so suited to me in every way; the leaving Woolwich, perhaps England, and all those I love so truly, and whose society and counsels have been so precious to my beloved wife and myself. It is grievous; but she, the true wife, smothers her own sorrow, and comforts me constantly by pointing to the love of Him who sends this trial, 'that we might be partakers of His holiness.' We are with the dear Rounds, who are all kindness and love.

"I have no strength to write more. We return home to-morrow. Ever—precious friend, mother, and sister—your own loving and grateful son and brother."

Up to this time, and even on the following Sabbath, he still persevered in going to church; and devoutly welcomed every opportunity of receiving the sacrament of the Lord's Supper.

On the 23rd of May, he went with Mrs Vandeleur, for change of air, to East Coombe, near Blackheath, the residence of his valued Christian friends, Mr and Mrs Mentor Mott. Here he was tended with the most considerate and affectionate care. His friends were painfully struck with his extreme weakness; and it was evident to them that he was rapidly sinking. From himself, it seemed, at this time, to be hidden. But those who loved him best, felt that this was a matter of no moment for one whose heart was filled with the Saviour's peace, and whose lips were continually breathing that Saviour's name. She who was just then bearing alone the burden of the dread of their approaching parting, was thankful for each day that his tender spirit was spared from fully realising the trial which was falling upon herself; strangely sad though it was, for the first time since their marriage, to bear a sorrow unshared and unsoothed by him.

On the 24th, Mrs Mott's sister, Mrs Thompson, (who has since devoted herself to a missionary labour of love amongst the Maronites,) drove over to Beckenham with Major Vandeleur; as he had set his heart on making arrangements for a visit to the Rectory early in the ensuing week, with the earnestness of an unacknowledged consciousness that he was coming to take a last long leave of friends who were, one and all, so deeply attached to him.

At that time, two beloved members of our family circle were seriously ill; but we all felt, alike, that nothing must be allowed to delay his visit.

On the morning of the 26th, whilst still at East Coombe, he awoke at sunrise with a sense of suffocation, and panting for breath. Mrs Vandeleur opened the window; and as the glorious rays of the rising sun fell around him, he raised his beaming eyes, exclaiming, "Oh for the blaze of the Sun of Righteousness!"

The next day was Whitsunday. It was a lovely morning; but his days for joining the worshippers in an earthly temple were over. His wife read part of the Service, and the Lessons, to him; and then they strolled out upon the lawn, and spent the remainder of the morning quietly there, amidst the calm of the sheltering trees, soft summer breezes, and still sunshine; taking sweet counsel together of the things that belonged to their everlasting peace. A treasured memory is that Sabbath morning, to the one who is left sorrowing on earth, and not forgotten, we believe, by the one who is bearing a victor's palm before the throne of the Lamb. In the afternoon, their friend Mrs Hare came to spend an hour with him; and an hour of delightful intercourse it proved to be. Several times Arthur referred to it, as having been to him a foretaste of the converse of Heaven.

The day before he left East Coombe, Mrs Vandeleur was obliged to return to Woolwich for an hour or two, and Mrs Thompson remained with him. He was unusually depressed, and after telling her that at times he believed that his end was near, the real source of his grief burst forth like a torrent, as he bitterly mourned over what he called "the uselessness of his life."

"What have I ever done for my Master? How I have wasted my opportunities! I am going to give an account of my stewardship, and what an account it must be!"

Mrs Thompson felt that this was but a device of the great enemy, to mar his peace; and endeavoured to comfort him by asking, if he could not remember any instance in which it had pleased God to bless his words to some poor sinner. His face brightened as she spoke, and, with expressions of the deepest thankfulness, he recalled, one by one, encouragements mercifully given to him by a gracious Master, and many instances in which He had made use of him to bring sinners to the foot of the Cross. He was at all times extremely silent on this subject, seldom speaking of it even to the one nearest and dearest to him. But we know that both his example and his words were widely blessed. Even in the short interval between the time when his death was known in Woolwich, and the day on which he was laid in his last resting-place, many testified with tears as to what he had been to them— the instrument in God's hands of bringing them to a knowledge of their Saviour.

The following morning, his kind and sympathising friend, Sir Richard Dacres, Commandant of the Garrison, and several of Arthur's brother-officers, came over from Woolwich, to see him. There was evidently an impression on the minds of all that it was for the last time.

Many non-commissioned officers and men also came to inquire after him; and some lingered about, hoping to catch another glimpse of one so well-beloved.

CHAPTER XVI.

The Last Sleep.

"So He giveth His beloved sleep."

"They say he died ;—it seem'd to me,
  That after hours of pain and strife,
He slept one evening peacefully,
  And woke in everlasting life."

JUST at the same season of the year, in which he had arrived at Beckenham Rectory, five years before, in joyous health and spirits, for his first visit on his return from the Crimea, Arthur came once more—a dying man. Yet, even then, it was almost impossible to associate with him, any thought that was not bright with life and hope. Again we heard that welcome sound of his clear, pleasant laugh, ending with a little shout of glee peculiar to himself. Again we found him ready for cheerful converse, happiest when it dwelt on the Christian's highest hopes, but ready to enter with zest into all that interested us.

Not allowing himself to fall into the usual ways of invalids, he joined the family circle at meal-times, excepting at breakfast only; and was not unmindful of any of the little courtesies of life. His early friend, Mr O'Donnell, might even have recalled that impression of Arthur's boyhood to which he alluded in his description of him :—" I thought him very careful of his personal appearance." Yet, mingling with the unconquered spirit, which seemed to triumph over the weakness and suffering of a dying illness, there was, at times, an almost childlike dependence, which his brave endurance only rendered the more deeply touching.

The last of May was a day of unbroken sunshine and soft westerly wind; and Arthur expressed a wish to sit on the lawn for an hour, under the shade of an old spreading chestnut-tree, which he had always particularly admired. It was my privilege to be his companion, during that time; for which I thank God to this day.

"I wished to ask you," he began, in a tone of deep solemnity, "whether it is possible that I may have been deceiving myself all along, in the belief that I have loved my Saviour. Now that I feel drawing near to death, I shrink from leaving that little tender, precious wife, and our sweet children, to battle with life without me. The thought of parting with them, in itself, is a terrible pang. Would this be so, if I had truly loved my Saviour? Should I not be longing to go to Him? Can I have deceived myself all along, in believing that I have loved Him?"

After a moment's pause for prayer, I replied, "Your safety, as you well know, does not depend upon your love for the Lord Jesus Christ, but upon His love for you. 'He loved you, and gave Himself for you.' And He has told you, 'He that heareth my word, and believeth on Him that sent me, *hath* everlasting life, and shall not come into condemnation; but *is passed* from death unto life.' If you had deceived yourself, in the time that is past, *He* can never deceive *you*. The life once given you through believing in Him—or, if you had never believed before, which would be given you *now*, as you believe 'His Word'—it is IMPOSSIBLE that He should withdraw, for any infirmity on your part. But my own entire conviction is, that that blessed Saviour—one of whose last thoughts, when dying to redeem a world, was for the comfort of His mother— far from deeming that there is unfaithfulness towards Him, in your tender love for your wife and children, would be much less pleased if you were so occupied with your own near prospect of immeasurable gain, as to forget the grievous loss which it must involve for them."

"Do you think so?" he said, his trustful spirit receiving the suggestion at once. "Oh, that is comfort indeed! And perhaps, after all, then I *do* love Him. For if the cry, ' Behold the Bridegroom cometh !' were to be sounded now, and I could go up, with Mary and our babes, to meet my Lord in the air, I should rejoice 'with joy unspeakable, and full of glory.'"

As he spoke, the colour flushed over his cheek, and his deep, spiritual eye, upraised to heaven, seemed to drink in fresh lustre from the Source of light. For a while he appeared to be unconscious of earthly companionship, in his fellowship of soul with his Lord and

Saviour. Like the saintly Rutherford, he seemed to say, "I only ask now a further revelation of the beauty of the unseen Son of God." With the prophet, he could say, in faith, Mine "eyes shall see the King in his beauty."

After a time, he turned to me, and said, "I want to speak of my mother, to one whom she would bless out of her holy heaven, for having so truly and tenderly represented her on earth to me, for five years." He then told me what she was to him in his childhood, and the history of their last interview, in minute detail. "I loved her as an angel of God," he said, "and I love her still, as entirely and devotedly as I did the day of her death. I have never ceased to miss her, and to mourn her."

After this, he spoke of the meeting before us all—which he believed to be drawing very near—the meeting in the air—to go in together to "the marriage-supper of the Lamb." Not the faintest doubt of mutual recognition there, crossed his mind. He spoke of those gone before, whom he had known and loved, as waiting to welcome him into Paradise. "I should not be surprised if 'Faithful'—that is Hedley, you know—would be one of those who will come to meet 'Hopeful' as he crosses Jordan," said he, alluding to a former half-playful comparison of Captain Vicars and himself to those beloved companions of Christian, in the "Pilgrim's Progress," on his way to the Celestial City.

I could but rejoin in Christian's words, " You have been Hopeful ever since I knew you."

" There is no such thing as death for a man who believes in the Saviour," he added. " He cannot die. He is in ' the Life,' for he is *in* Jesus; and thus he is a part of Life Eternal."

Whilst thus speaking, his brother-in-law, Mr Charles Molony, arrived from Woolwich; and I left them alone together for a few minutes; thankful for the opportunity of withdrawing to bless God for having permitted me to hear, from this beloved friend, so glorious a confession of faith.

During the following day, he had further conversation with Mr Chalmers, whom his eyes often followed with a wistful look when he was called from the room by parish duties ; and he liked to have his chair placed, in the evening, where he could best see my father's serene and beautiful countenance. " I cannot make my voice heard through his trumpet now," he said to me, rather sadly; then brightening again immediately, " but we shall have plenty of time for talking together, when we meet in the everlasting Home."

Interested, to the last, for the welfare of the soldier, he collected donations on that day, as on several previous days, for the Soldiers' Institute at Woolwich ; and he carried back thither the sum of £30, to keep it going. Regarding it as a great benefit for the men, he was most anxious that the Institute should be placed upon a permanent foundation.

In the night-time, latterly, he frequently prayed in his broken sleep. He awoke very early; and if his tender and devoted wife—herself looking scarcely less fragile than he—who watched him unweariedly through his wakeful hours, had closed her eyes for brief repose after seeing him fall asleep, he would quietly rise to light the fire, rather than disturb her whom he so anxiously cared for, and so deeply loved; or even than ring, at that early hour, for the aid of a servant.

He dreaded giving the least trouble. But the last night or two, from extreme weakness and breathlessness, he submitted to being assisted to his room by a dear young friend—himself a soldier—then staying with us, to whom Arthur's heart had warmed from their first interview; and by a faithful servant of Mr Chalmers, who had loved him with no common love. But readily and tenderly as this little service was performed, and much as he prized the love which rendered it, it was an evident pain to him to be obliged to avail himself of it.

On Friday, he said to me, " I should like to go to Heaven straight from this dear home. But whilst your beloved sister and niece are so ill, I feel it is wrong to add a third invalid to the house. I mean to go back to Woolwich to-day, to see my little children ; and then Mary and I will come again, in a few days, and stay to the *end*. And the end will be the beginning of glory."

He hoped, then, that he should return. But I do not think that he believed it, a few hours later, when he parted from us. My sister, who had been suffering from an attack of bronchitis, had risen that afternoon for the sake of getting a last glimpse of one who was so dear to her, and to us all. When he looked up, and saw her sorrowful face watching him from the gallery as he crossed the hall, the tender solemnity of a last farewell overspread his countenance; and as he entered the carriage, he hid his face, in a sudden burst of tears.

The next day, he began to complain of great pain in his throat, and seemed weaker, and less able to exert himself. In the evening he said, "What a blessing, my Mary, that I have not *now to seek* Jesus!"

On Sunday, he rallied considerably, and was again able to converse, fully and clearly. In the course of the morning, he spoke to his wife of his approaching death, and then said to her, "Come and sit by my side, and speak to me about it. I shall realise it if *you* talk of it; I do not, when others allude to it." She drew a low chair to his side, and sat by him, calmly speaking of that which was to bring her own deepest sorrow. He said, "It is a solemn thing to appear before the King of kings—the Holy God; but I have *no* fear;" and then expressed his perfect trust, and peace, and joy in Jesus, as his own and all-suffi-cient Saviour.

That afternoon, his beloved brother, Captain Trevor Molony, read a sermon to him, which he much enjoyed, on his favourite words, "CHRIST IS ALL."

Soon afterwards, his kind friend, Colonel Tulloh, who had shewn him the truest sympathy throughout his illness, and his dear friends, Captain Bruce and Captain Hutchinson, called to inquire after him. He was able to see Colonel Tulloh and Captain Bruce, who came the earliest; and they found that he was quite cheerful in manner and conversation.

On Tuesday, the 5th of June, his sister, Mrs Carden, arrived. She found that, for the first time, he had felt himself too weak to rise from his bed. On perceiving the great change in him, she could not restrain her tears. He raised his eyes, so full of the peace of Jesus, and said, with the most earnest tenderness, "O Louie, don't cry for me. I am going home. I have long known that in my Father's house there is a place prepared for me. I know it—I am sure of it. Do you know, dearest sister, that there is a place prepared for *you?* If you do not certainly know it, never rest, never cease to agonize in prayer till the assurance is given you."

In the afternoon, he seemed tolerably easy, and was very animated. Captain Molony, whose presence and sympathy were amongst the chief comforts of his long illness, was sitting by his side, and then Arthur asked for something pleasant to be read to him; and smiling at his wife, added, "I wish to be amused, Mary!"

In the evening he was much exhausted, and spoke very little. But twice he was heard to repeat the words, "JESUS ONLY"—as if all other lights were paling before the everlasting day, just dawning for him, when the Sun of Righteousness should arise and shed its glories upon his soul for ever, without a cloud between.

About eleven o'clock at night, he asked his wife to read to him the 19th chapter of the Gospel of St Luke; which he seemed greatly to enjoy, making remarks upon some of the verses.

At one o'clock, the lonely watcher by his side, scarcely able to see him in the shaded light, knew by his gentle breathing that he had fallen asleep; and he seemed to sleep so peacefully, that she began to have a trembling hope that he might awake refreshed and better.

But that quiet sleeper awoke not. As the sun arose that morning, it shone upon the face of the dead. Without one pang of parting, his mortal life had been exchanged for Immortality. He had fallen asleep in Jesus,—" the Life of them that believe, and the Resurrection of the dead."

*   *   *   *   *

So, when the Christian's eyelid droops and closes,
    In nature's parting strife,
A friendly angel stands where he reposes,
    To take him up to life.

He gives a gentle blow, and so releases
    The spirit from its clay;
From sins, temptations, and from life's distresses,
    He bids it "Come away."

It rises up, and from its darksome mansion
    It takes its silent flight,
And feels its freedom in the large expansion
    Of Heavenly Light.

Behind! it hears Time's iron gates close faintly;
    It is now far from them,
For it has reach'd the city of the saintly—
    "The New Jerusalem."

The voice is heard on earth of kinsfolk weeping
    The loss of one they love;
But he is gone where the redeem'd are keeping
    "A Festival of Love."

The mourners throng the ways, and from the steeple
    The funeral bell tolls slow;
But on the golden streets the holy people
    Are passing to and fro;

And saying as they meet, "Rejoice! another
    Long waited for is come!"
The Saviour's heart is glad; a younger brother
    Hath reach'd the Father's Home.

THE CAMERA;

OR,

THE BELIEVER CHANGED INTO THE IMAGE OF HIS SAVIOUR.*

> "But we all, with open face beholding as in a glass the glory of the Lord, are changed into the same image from glory to glory, even as by the Spirit of the Lord."—2 Cor. iii. 18.

One of the most striking features in those discourses of our blessed Lord, to the multitudes who flocked to listen to the gracious words that proceeded out of His mouth, of which short summaries are handed down to us in the Gospels, is the elegant simplicity of the language He invariably employed.

He well knew, not only the exact circumstances of every soul that heard Him, but also the power of mind, the grasp of memory, and the amount of education, possessed by each individual. This He knew when Pharisees and doctors of the law sat by, and when even the highest in the land listened to Him gladly. How eloquent, pointed, and appropriate was

---

* This address was found, with many others of the same kind, among the papers of Major Vandeleur, and is printed as a specimen of the lectures which he was in the habit of delivering to the soldiers at Woolwich.

T

His language on such occasions ! yet how simple — how easy to be understood ! And the reason of this is obvious. The great majority of His hearers were the ignorant, uneducated, uncared-for poor ; and He who was anointed to preach the gospel to the poor, took good care to convey the glad tidings of salvation to their minds in language so simple and beautiful, as could not possibly be misunderstood by the weakest mind among them desirous of being taught.

It is well known that every truth which weak minds can comprehend is perfectly intelligible to those of greater power. In speaking, then, to the uninformed and illiterate, in language suited to their capacities, not only did our Lord convey His meaning to all the rest of His audience ; but, with that infinite wisdom which pertains to the great Creator of all things, He considered the wants and capabilities of generations to come throughout the whole world ; and, looking forward to the time when the gracious words which proceeded out of His mouth should be translated into the languages of heathen and savage as well as of civilised nations, He made use of such symbols and illustrations as are well known and familiar to all the nations of the earth as well as to the Jews. And then, having fixed the minds of His hearers on the material scene, (probably in many cases existing, or being enacted before their eyes,) He made use of their natural senses for impressing on their memories the important spiritual truths which He designed to teach them. It was thus that He turned the daily and ordinary occurrences of life into spiritual food for famishing souls. It is probable that, while the parable of the sower fell from His lips, the eyes of the multitude frequently changed from the person of our blessed Lord himself to the figure of the husbandman pursuing his work in the distance.

It is probable also, that the parables of the vine and its branches, the sheepfold, the householder hiring labourers in the market-place, and most of His other parables, were either suggested by the circumstances of the moment, or that He waited for an opportune instant, not only to point out the close connexion between natural and revealed religion, but also to fix their attention powerfully on the great truths which formed the subject of His discourse, by making their outward senses contribute to the development of the correct idea in their minds, instead of (as is too often the case amongst ourselves) having quite the contrary effect. And further, He might intend that whenever a similar scene, under similar circumstances, was presented to their view, it should recall His weighty and solemn words, and so cause them to be stored up in their memories and bring forth fruit unto life eternal.

Though these discourses of our Lord Jesus Christ are the most striking and forcible examples extant of this mode of teaching, still it was not altogether new to His Jewish hearers,—the same Divine Spirit which spake in Him having dictated a similar mode of expression to the prophets and fathers of old. Moses, David, Isaiah, and Jeremiah, all made use of material symbols to convey their meaning ; and David, in some of the most beautiful of his psalms, only turns to spiritual profit an event of every-day life. I need only refer, for illustration, to the 23rd and 42nd Psalms, where, in the one case, a shepherd leading his flock, and in the other, a tired hart panting after the water-brook, suggest a series of meditations delightful to read, but still more delightful to experience.

In our own day, too, the best and most successful writers depend much upon similitudes, in working out their happiest ideas. Wilberforce, in his " Practical View," when wishing to express his conviction of the necessity of minds of great power submitting implicitly to the declarations of the in- spired Word of God, compares the Bible to the grass of the field. As the latter is food alike for the greatest as well as the least animal in creation, so is the Bible for the greatest as well as for the weakest mind. But the grass is food for large animals only on condition that they *bow the head;* and, by analogy, he argues that the mightiest intellect should receive unhesitatingly as truth whatever God declares, though beyond its power to comprehend. I will mention only one other instance. When anxious to express the awful facility with which the remembrance of the uncertainty of life passes from the mind, one of our most terse and power-ful poets, Dr Young, uses these expressions :—

> " As from the wing no scar the sky retains,
> The parted wave no furrow from the keel,
> So dies in human hearts the thought of death."

In accordance, therefore, with our blessed Master's mode of argument, I propose to draw your attention to some important truths, through the medium of a similitude.

Among the recent discoveries of science, there is none which has made such rapid progress towards perfection, or contributed so powerfully to the social comfort and happiness of millions, as the art of photography.

But few years have elapsed since Daguerre discovered that certain substances, such as the iodide of silver, are so sensitive to light as to be influenced by, and permanently to retain, the pictures presented to them in the camera obscura. The subject was at once seen to be of such vast importance as to induce the ablest chemists of both Europe and America to turn their attention to it. Their patient investigations and reasonings have been followed by, if not complete, still at least very great success. Many *known* substances have been ascertained to be of great value to the art, and others, pre-viously *unknown*, have sprung into permanent existence. The operations or manipulations of the art are so simple, that success is sure to attend the steps of the patient, persevering artist,—a rigid attention to the rules and formulas laid down, and a certain amount of manual dexterity, being all that is required. It is these circumstances, combined with the rapidity of the operation, which has placed photographic pictures within reach of the humblest in the land ; and it is their extraordinary faithfulness and truth which makes them such favourites with all classes.

We may well ask, " From whence do these characteristics come ?" Chiefly because the result is so much the work of *nature*, so little that of *man ;* for man merely places the substances, of which he has discovered some properties, in circumstances favourable for the development of those properties, and leaves the rest to nature, or to nature's God. In this respect it somewhat resembles the seed sown in the earth. If we take seed of any description, and sow it at the proper season in soil suited to it, manure, watch, and weed it ; in due course of time—nature being left to follow its inviolable laws in the interval—we reap the fruit of our labours. In this case, man might as properly claim to himself the credit of having produced several ears of corn from a single grain, as imagine that the wonderful truthfulness, minuteness, and beauty of the photograph, resulting from his work, is due to his skilful manipulation. No ; it is God's work. He merely makes use of man as an instrument, and to Him we should invariably give the praise. It is thus that the Almighty works in everything that man does. While we lay out plans for our own action, whether individual or social, God is the great guiding Spirit ; and whether we succeed or fail in accomplishing that which we proposed to effect, everything that we have done is made use of by Infinite Wisdom and Power for the furtherance of His own great plans of love and mercy. In fact, every great mental and social stride which man has accomplished in the progress of the world towards civilisation, has also been a step in furtherance of Christianity.

The art of printing is a remarkable proof of the truth of this position. It is supposed to have been discovered by Lawrence Costa about the year 1442, and was introduced by Caxton into England about 1471. From this period till the commencement of the Reformation in Germany, by the posting of Luther's ninety-five theses on the walls of Wittenburg in 1517, was only forty-six years. This period we may easily

suppose to have been just sufficient to bring the art to a forward state ; and when thus perfect and ready for its work, it
was made use of by Infinite Wisdom to multiply immensely
the number of copies of the Holy Scriptures in the world,
and thus defeat the designs of Satan, and push forward the
great work of Reformation in the Church.   A moment's
reflection would suffice to convince us that the discovery of
the mariner's compass, the art of navigation, and the power of
steam, have all tended remarkably to forward what we know
to be the grand design of Jehovah, the infinite God, in His
management of the world as it exists at present,—viz., the
salvation of sinful man by the death of His Son ; and to this
end the sciences of astronomy, chemistry, and geology, have
all given most valuable aid ; whether we regard them as
exposing the false theories and dreadful delusions of all false
religions, or as confirming and illustrating, directly and indi-
rectly, the infallible statements of Holy Writ.

Thus, for instance, astronomy exalts and enlarges our ideas
of the power and glory of the Triune Jehovah, by proving
that this world, so stupendous to our eyes, is but a little
speck in comparison with the millions of suns and worlds
which He has created by His Word, and preserves for ever in
their station and circuit in accordance with His will.

Chemistry reveals to us many of the hidden wonders of the
material world, explains to us the reasons and objects of the
marvellous changes that are incessantly going on around us, and
shews how God, with smallest means, effects the noblest ends.

Geology, searching out the inmost recesses and depths of
the globe we inhabit, points out the order, design, and system
which prevail there ; confirms most strikingly the Mosaic
account of the formation and arrangement of the present
order of things above, around, below us ; and lends its powerful aid in corroboration of the statements of our blessed Lord
Jesus Christ, as well as of St Peter, and others of the sacred
writers, who have foretold that it shall surely come to pass
" that the heavens, being on fire, shall be dissolved, and the

elements shall melt with fervent heat, the earth also, and the things that are therein, shall be burnt up." It shews how easily, by means of agencies now in active operation within the earth's crust, merely by a sudden increase of that activity, all these prophecies *may*—how much in accordance with former occurrences on our globe it is that they *should*—how probable it is that they WILL—be performed! And, by pointing out the tremendous and heart-appalling character which this event will assuredly assume, it speaks most strongly to each soul. Oh that we may all listen to its voice! Flee from the wrath to come,—close with the easy terms which God offers,—" escape for thy life,"—" escape to the mountain," the sinner's only refuge, Jesus Christ,—" lest thou be consumed."

As yet, the art of photography can hardly be considered to have contributed to the progress of the gospel. But we cannot doubt, judging from analogy, that God will, in His own good time and way, cause an art which is already practised in every country of the world, and will soon be universally known, to lend its powerful aid to urge forward the cause of Christianity and peace. The way in which it may please Almighty God to do this, I pretend not to explain, or even to conjecture.

The use I propose to make of photography to-day, is to furnish a symbol or series of comparisons between the manipulations of the art and the operations of God's grace in the soul of a sinner, in bringing him to a knowledge of the work of Christ for him, and making him fit and meet to be a partaker of the inheritance of the saints in light.

And may the Holy Spirit of our God deign graciously to bless the words which shall be spoken, and so to impress upon the souls of all who hear, the absolute necessity of the new birth, *as regards themselves*, while yet there is time, that in the day of Christ's appearing to judge the world, you may every one of you be found among the number of those who, being clad in the spotless robe of Christ's righteousness, and having on the wedding garment, shall be counted worthy to enter in to the marriage supper of the Lamb !

It is desirable that I should first describe, in as general terms as possible, the ordinary mode of manipulation in use among photographers, in order that the similitude which I shall subsequently draw may be thoroughly understood.

There are two processes which produce strikingly successful results. In the first, that of the daguerreotype, the sensitive surface which is to receive the picture is formed on a metal plate, generally copper, coated with silver; in the other, it is formed on a thin layer of a substance called " collodion," stretched on a glass plate. The latter is the cheaper and more ordinary mode, and I propose to allude to it alone.

The camera, or instrument in which the pictures are taken, is, as most of you are aware, a box, nearly square, and stained black on the inside. The lens, or glass through which the image is transmitted, is fixed at one end of this box, and in a brass cylinder. The frame, containing the sensitive plate, is, when the plate is ready, placed in this box opposite to the lens. When the slide is in its place, and the lens is covered, the inside is perfectly dark. On the cover of the lens being removed, light enters, and only through this medium. The construction of this glass lens is such, that the rays of light which enter are those only which are reflected from the object placed opposite at suitable distance ; these rays, falling upon the sensitive plate, there form a picture of that object exactly as it exists. Some parts are light, others of a medium shade, and others again quite dark ; and the plate being affected by the light in exact proportion to its *intensity*, it follows that the picture will exhibit corresponding degrees of light and shade.

The mode of preparing the plate to receive the impression is as follows :—

After being thoroughly cleaned, some collodion is poured over the surface, and the surplus drained off. The volatile liquid part having evaporated, which it does almost immediately, it is then placed in the sensitising bath ; after remaining there a few minutes, it is transferred to the frame, and carried to its position in the camera, which has previously been directed and focussed on the object to be taken.

An exposure of a few seconds or minutes is sufficient to effect the required change. The frame and plate are then returned to the developing-room ; and when *first* taken out of the frame, not the slightest vestige of a change can be discovered on the surface of the plate.

The application of the developing solution produces a speedy change, and resemblance to the object taken may at once be traced ; the resemblance becomes more and more decided, till the operation has been carried on to the proper point. This liquid is then washed off, and another applied, the effect of which, though quite dissimilar to that previously used, is essential to the perfection of the picture. It removes all the parts of the opaque film which have not been affected by the light, and which now tend *only to obscure the image.* It is called the fixing solution, and when the surplus of this has been removed, the picture is completed.

The resemblance between these details, and the work of grace in the soul, may not at first sight appear obvious ; but a little reflection will enable us to discover many and beautiful points of similarity. It will be remembered that the plate, covered with its collodion film, was at first perfectly *insensible* to the strongest light. It required a certain definite operation to be performed, and when that had been effected it became *sensitive to the faintest ray.* The condition of the plate, previous to this operation, fitly illustrates the condition of man by nature. The gospel may have been proclaimed in his hearing a thousand times ; he may have been a regular attendant on divine ordinances ; may never have been absent from his seat in the house of God ; may have much head-knowledge of the truth ; may be strictly correct in his moral conduct, and a highly esteemed member of society,—and yet all this time he may remain ignorant of Christ, be living without God in the world, a child of wrath, and in danger of eternal damnation. Why is this ? Because his heart has never been touched, never been " sensitised " by the Holy Spirit. But when this has been done—mark, what a change ! The man now sees things in a new light, discovers how severe are the requirements of God's law—how utterly hopeless it is for him ever, by any amount of self-denial or other works, to work out his own salvation. He now sees that having once failed (though it were but for a moment) to keep the first commandment in all its integrity, which commands him " to love the Lord his God with all his heart, and with all his soul, and with all his mind," (Matt. xxii. 37,) " he is guilty of all." A moment's recollection serves to convince him that he has failed in this, not only for a single moment, but for whole days and even years of his life.   He must then look out of himself for salvation—and where shall he turn to ? No mere mortal can save him, for God, he knows, has said that " none of them can by any means redeem his brother, nor give to God a ransom for him," (Ps. xlix. 7 ;) and finding at last that there is no hope for him but in Christ, and being now most anxious to obtain eternal life, he flees at once to Christ, casts himself at the foot of the cross, and on his knees, in secret, implores the pardon of his sins that are past ; he desires to be made a child of God, and begs for the gift of the Holy Spirit to enable him to lead a new life.

This brings us to the second point of the simile. The plate during the process of sensitising, and while the picture is being impressed upon it in the camera, as well as during the time of developing and fixing, has carefully to be shielded from light and external influences ; in fact, all the various operations, from the commencement of the picture to its completion, have to be performed in the dark room, and in the dark camera. May not this suggest to us *the Christian's closet—his place of prayer*—where, alone with God, he pours out his inmost thoughts, confesses his sins, and implores forgiveness ? Here, too, it is that God makes known His will to His child, reveals Christ to his soul in all the fulness of His infinite love, imparts fresh supplies of grace, and strengthens his heart to fight the good fight of faith against his powerful spiritual enemies. In fact, the Christian's closet may be considered as the workshop of the Almighty, where He prepares His servant to work for Him here below, and fits him for heaven hereafter.

My dear friends, when speaking upon this subject, I cannot forbear urging upon your most serious and earnest consideration the importance and necessity of prayer. It is not that I would for one moment underrate the value of other Christian duties and observances. God forbid ! But that I would now wish to raise in your estimation, and fix in your memories, the obligation and privilege of *prayer*. It is a sure sign of spiritual life. Does any soul that listens to me, know in himself that he is constantly at the throne of grace, and that his supplications there, offered up in his Saviour's name, are humble and earnest ? Let him take comfort. His feet are surely on the Rock of Ages, and though perhaps now cast down and ready to despair, let him continue as he has begun. The Lord Jehovah will perfect that which concerneth him, He will never forsake the work of His own hands.

On the other hand,—does any one, who has seemed to be a believer in the Lord Jesus, feel within himself that he is different from what he was ; that now his prayers are less frequent and shorter than they used to be ; that he does not take so much delight as he once did in bending before the throne of grace ; that his prayers are more formal and less earnest ? Oh, my brother, or sister, beware, I beseech you. Satan is desirous of having you, that he may sift you as wheat. He has taken new and firmer hold on your heart. He has wounded you grievously in a vital point. Let me exhort you, again, instantly to return unto the Lord. Confess your wandering ; repent and do your first works, lest your candlestick be removed out of its place, and you perish for ever. "Return unto the Lord, and He will have mercy upon you ; and to your God, for He will abundantly pardon."

In truth, dear friends, it would be impossible for me, or any other mortal, to overrate the value and importance of prayer. It is not only a sign of spiritual life, but it is the authorised channel in which flow all good and perfect gifts to the soul of man. A Christian poet has well expressed its importance in that beautiful hymn—

> " Prayer was appointed to convey
>   The blessings God design'd to give.
> Long as they live should Christians pray,
>   For only while they pray they live.
>
> " Prayer is the Christian's vital breath,
>   The Christian's native air,
> His watchword at the gates of death ;
>   He enters heaven by prayer."

To prove that these statements are not made without scriptural authority, I need only refer you to St Paul's injunction to the Philippians—" In everything by prayer and supplication with thanksgiving, let your requests be made known unto God." And also to our Lord's own precepts and promises in regard to prayer—" Ask, and it shall be given you ; seek, and ye shall find ; knock, and it shall be opened unto you." " Whatsoever ye shall ask in my name, that will I do, that the Father may be glorified in the Son." And even more in accordance with the point under consideration—" But thou, when thou prayest, enter into thy closet, and when thou hast shut thy door, pray to thy Father which is in secret, and thy Father which seeth in secret, shall reward thee openly."

I need hardly explain to you, that whatever place the Christian chooses for secret prayer, *that* is the Christian's closet. Under the ever-varying circumstances of life, seasons must occur when it is quite impossible for us to separate ourselves completely from our fellow-creatures, even for a short time. We may be so poor as to occupy a single room in common with many others. We may be on board ship, in a railway train, or in a crowded tent ; but under all these, or indeed under any possible circumstances in which we may be placed, it is quite possible for us to be alone with our heavenly Father, and to enjoy communion with Him. That young sailor well understood the spirit of our Saviour's command, who said, when on board a crowded man-of-war, that, on the eve of battle, he had spent an hour alone with his God in the crown of his cap. Oh, how many of us ought to blush when we compare such noble conduct with our own ; when we remember how easily we suffer little trifles to interfere with the time which should be given to God by us every day !

But the Christian's time in his closet is not altogether spent in prayer. He there reads God's sacred Word, and meditates thereon ; he strives to ascertain what God would have him to believe, and what to do, and what to leave undone. And his search is never in vain. As, when the plate is uncovered in the camera, the rays from the object placed before it pass through the lens and, falling upon it, effect the change that is required, even so God, through the glass of His Holy Word, presents Christ to his soul, makes him to see and know something of the length and breadth and depth and height of His infinite love. Not all at once, but gradually, He unfolds to him the surpassing beauty and perfection of the perfect man—Christ Jesus; and while constantly viewing His spotless and spiritual character, the believer is himself gradually conformed to the likeness of Christ; so that others do now take knowledge of him that he has been with Jesus ; or as the words of our text beautifully express the same thought, *making use of this very image:* "But we all, with open face beholding as in a glass the glory of the Lord, are changed into the same image from glory to glory, even as by the Spirit of the Lord." Yes, as in the case of the photograph, all has to be done in the dark room ; so in the instance of the believer, it is when apart from the world, and alone with God, that Christ is presented to his view, through the glass of His Holy Word. It is in the closet that *the image is developed;* it is in the closet that it is perfected. True, external circumstances may be, and often are, the means which God employs both to build up His child in the faith, and afterwards to purge out all the old leaven which still clings so close to him, and seems so likely for ever to mar the image of his blessed Lord ; *but it is not until these external circumstances, whether sickness, or bereavement, or trial, or persecution, or whatever else they may be, are brought into the workshop, are pondered over, are prayed over, are made to sink into the soul, are seen as coming from God's hands for some special purpose;* it is not, I say, until these external circumstances are brought into the closet, that they prove of any use or value towards perfecting the Christian character of the child of God.

Then, dear friends, let me from this take occasion to urge you seriously to let all your external circumstances and matters of everyday life be made by you, individually, subjects of private meditation and prayer. All [illegible]gs which happen to us are ordered of God for us, and He d[illegible] not order things without reason. Nay, He has great and [illegible]reaso[illegible] or even the trifles which occur in daily life. T[illegible] we attend to those trifles, and endeavour to see God's h[illegible]d in them, not only will the attempt be successful ; but if [illegible] obey *the indications of His will thus afforded*, we may s[illegible]selves *many great and sore troubles.* If we suffer ours[illegible] be guided by His eye, He will lead us gently ; we s[illegible] need His chastening hand to be laid heavily upon u[illegible]r, to use the words of Scripture, shall we require to be r[illegible]ained by bit and bridle, like horse and mule.

These are the chief points of the resemblance. I might also trace many minor ones.

For instance, the slightest speck of dust getting on the plate considerably mars, and may even destroy the whole picture ; and thousands of pictures are daily destroyed in this way.

Oh, how many fair Christian characters has one sin blighted ! Let us beware lest it be so with us,—the stain must be removed, the darling sin must be renounced and abandoned, or we perish for ever.

Again, a weak picture is useless, or almost so, for taking impressions from, or making similar pictures. From a strong "negative," as it is technically termed, any number may be taken. The weak picture is only valuable to be itself set in a frame.

So with Christians, it is the strong, earnest, confirmed Christians that are chiefly made use of as instruments in God's hand for the conversion of other souls. But the simple, weak brother, though not made use of so openly, still glorifies God by his holy life and conversation, and will doubtless shine as a jewel in our glorious Saviour's crown.

Lastly, Even with the rapid strides which this wonderful art has made, how inferior is the picture to the original from which it was taken! How poor, how feeble, how harsh, how diminutive! How exactly the type of the Christian, even the most advanced and holy Christian, as compared with His glorious pattern, his Divine Original! But as, in the one case, we look forward to the time when the power of transferring through the camera, not only the outlines of the object, *but the colours also*, shall arrive: so on the other, we Christians are justified in looking forward to the coming time, when we shall be with Him near, and like our God ; when we shall see Him face to face, and know even as also we are known. May this be the happy lot, the blessed portion of each soul now present, for Jesus Christ our Saviour's sake! Amen.

THE END.

www.ingramcontent.com/pod-product-compliance
Lightning Source LLC
Chambersburg PA
CBHW031044120726
47905CB00007B/2304